Enjoy the journey,
Karen!

Mark Butterworth

THE
FFRYES
AFFAIR

W0018959

MC BUTTERWORTH

The
Book
Guild

First published in Great Britain in 2025 by
The Book Guild Ltd
Unit E2 Airfield Business Park,
Harrison Road, Market Harborough,
Leicestershire. LE16 7UL
Tel: 0116 2792299
www.bookguild.co.uk
Email: info@bookguild.co.uk
X: @bookguild

Typeset in 10pt Adobe Garamond Pro

Printed and bound in Great Britain by 4edge Limited

ISBN 978 1835741 238

British Library Cataloguing in Publication Data.
A catalogue record for this book is available from the British Library.

To Mike and Lisa

ONE

She wore a light blue cotton dress that fitted closely, but not tightly, to her tall, slim figure. She was once told that her best feature was her beautiful green eyes, which she now emphasised with just a touch of mascara. A light pink lipstick was sufficient to complete the professional executive look. Antonia had chosen a green and white Ferragamo silk scarf, lightly knotted around her neck, and white leather sandals with a low heel, which gave her the posture she liked but without seeming to be power dressing. Her auburn hair was in a French twist – a style she had been given as a young child by her grandmother. Since it had suited her so well, she had stayed with it, regardless of changing fashions. She felt ready for her first day at her new job. With just a touch of apprehension, she checked herself in the mirror and took a deep breath.

"Let's go," she said, then stepped outside and locked the door.

Her flat was on the upper floor of a modern two-storey block close to a golf course. She walked along the balcony and stopped at the top of the external staircase to take in the view across Jolly Harbour. Tall sailing yacht masts crowded together, multi-million-dollar cruisers were tied up in their own berths and a couple of inflatable tenders were puttering into the marina. Although it was only a five-minute walk from her flat to the Ministry of Tourism, Antonia left at quarter to nine, even though she knew she would be a little early for her nine o'clock start time. *Being early is much better than being even a minute late on your first day*, she thought.

She glanced into the offices and restaurants that lined the harbour. Grouper Marine, the largest chandlery on the island, stood centre stage, alongside insurance brokers, finance companies, yacht charter agencies, and property letting and sales agents' offices – all vital to meet the needs of the wealthy and super-rich. She noticed a car rental agency, a beauty salon and a hairdressers. At the far end of the street, she could just see the front of the Gourmand supermarket. She made a mental note to call in after work – she needed to buy some food to supplement the starter pack that the rental agents had provided.

The bars and restaurants that lined the marina boardwalk looked so enticing, with outside seating, colourful paintwork in shades of blue, yellow and red, and woven straw sunshades. She put all thoughts of relaxing with a drink out of her mind as she reached the entrance to the Antigua and Barbuda Ministry of Tourism.

When Antonia stepped inside, she was greeted by Florence, the head of marketing, who Antonia recognised from photos she had seen on the ministry's website. Antonia guessed that Florence was in her late twenties; tall and elegant, she walked like a model. Antonia was stunned by Florence's good looks: she had deep mahogany eyes and the most engaging, welcoming smile. She looked stylish in a long, slim green and red dress with a pattern of leaves and tropical flowers, and a matching turban. She eagerly held out her hand in greeting.

"Good morning, Antonia! I'm Florence Prideaux. Welcome to the island and you are especially welcome to the Ministry of Tourism. It's lovely to meet you."

"And to meet you, Florence. Thank you, it's great to be here at last. What plans do you have for me today?"

"Oh, we have lots of fun things lined up. Mr Aaron Jaygo, the director of tourism, will be here shortly and he will update you on the latest elements of the tourism strategy for the islands. I understand you met him during your interview process on one of your flights to Antigua. I will introduce you to all the staff – we have a team of eight people, including us. Then, later this morning, we will go for a walking tour of Jolly Harbour. This afternoon, we have set up a meeting with the Antigua Hotels Association general manager and her assistant. She will outline how they plan to develop wider international interest in tourism here and on Barbuda. They are very keen to meet you! You are our very first tourism planning manager, so you can understand their excitement."

"Excellent. Sounds like quite a full day," said Antonia.

"Yes, there is certainly plenty of work for us. We have so much catching up to do since the Covid crisis. You may be aware that we had a really tough time during the lockdown." Florence's smile faded as she described the unemployment and financial hardship experienced throughout the islands. "Most of the hotels, retailers, import and export firms – in fact everyone involved in the tourism sector – laid off most of their staff and there was very little government support. Certainly no furlough payments or anything like that. People had to rely on help from relatives and their communities to even buy food."

"It must have been awful." Antonia was shaken by the image. She hadn't realised how fragile the tourism industry and therefore the island's economy was.

"But we're bouncing back and next year we expect to exceed all previous years in visitor numbers!" Florence was smiling again. "Come on, let me show you to your desk."

***

The day flew by. Just before 5 p.m. Florence suggested a sundowner at the Mango Tree bar, a few steps along the boardwalk. Antonia was delighted to accept. She felt she could do with a drink and it would be a great opportunity to get to know Florence a little better. As they settled into their seats in the shade, Florence opened the cocktail menu with a flourish.

"Now then, let's see what we have here. Anything you fancy?"

Antonia had the feeling that Florence knew the list back to front. "Please, you order for me. Something with white rum would be nice."

"Good choice. I have just the thing for you – and you know what? I'm going to have the same. They do a lovely watermelon daiquiri here."

"Sounds delicious – really Caribbean! Florence, do you live in Jolly Harbour?"

"Not exactly. My house is about a fifteen-minute walk towards St John's. It's a beautifully restored villa and I live there with my mother. We are very lucky that Father owned one of the tourist shops at the cruise terminal – it sold watches and jewellery. He left a substantial legacy for me and I bought the house just last year."

The barman came to their table. "Good evening, Miss Prideaux. What can I get you and your guest tonight?"

Antonia was impressed by the man's politeness and welcoming style. Florence ordered drinks and requested some olives, pretzels and a selection of tapas plates.

The sound of laughter came from the bar, where a group had gathered. Some sat on high stools; others stood in a broad semi-circle. Antonia unconsciously turned to look, raised her eyebrows and smiled at Florence.

"They're mostly British expats, some American and Canadian, living in the harbour villas you can see across the water," said Florence.

"Some are regular visitors to the island and they have got to know the locals. They all meet up around five, have a few drinks and maybe eat in one of the restaurants."

"Sounds like a great life."

"Well, yes, if you like that sort of thing. I'm not sure I would go for it myself. You can easily get tied into a cliquey group. There's not much else for them to do in the evening."

"Do most of them have jobs here?"

Florence couldn't resist a smile. "Ah, no. Some do, a few charter out their yacht or have some business interest in property and tourism. The tall lady in the white dress runs a boutique in Heritage Quay, near the cruise terminal. Cotton and linen dresses and silver jewellery, handmade on the island – that sort of thing. She does very well, but most of those folk are living off their pensions. There will be nothing left for the grandchildren!"

They both laughed.

Antonia leant forward. "Yes, as much as it's enjoyable having an occasional drink with other expats after work, that's not something I came to the island for. This is a career move for me. I intend to work hard, deliver the role I've taken on, and try and stay fit!"

"That's always a challenge, but there's a gym here in Jolly Harbour. Membership is included for all ministry employees. And there are plenty of safe places to swim. Some beaches are nicer than others; just let me know where you plan to go. And of course, it's best not to be out on your own after dark."

"Really? I thought Antigua was a safe place to live." There was more tension in Antonia's voice than she intended.

"Oh yes, it is, relatively. We have a low crime rate, but, like anywhere in the world, you should be cautious when you're out on your own."

"I'm sure you're right. Thank you."

Without being asked, the barman brought two more watermelon

daiquiris to their table, with the message that Eric, the owner, sent his compliments and would like to welcome Miss Antonia Casey-Brown to the island.

Antonia was visibly taken aback at the waiter knowing her name and she hadn't even met the owner. "Send my thanks, please. That's very kind."

"I certainly will, Miss Casey-Brown."

"There you are," said Florence. "Island life – everybody knows what's going on!"

***

After showering and getting ready for bed, Antonia sat at the small desk in her room and poured a glass of water. The evening was warm and humid, but the air con in her flat was very effective. She could hear tree frogs chirping and the regular ching-ching of ropes tapping against masts on the yachts in the marina. Antonia spent some time reading the papers that Florence had given her on tourist profiles, the countries people came from, how long they stayed, how much they spent. She was excited about getting to grips with the job ahead. She knew it was not going to be easy, devising and implementing a tourism plan that would make a real difference to the islands – and the islanders – but she had a range of ideas that she would discuss with her boss, Aaron, in the coming days.

Antonia had sent an 'I'm here!' text to her mother and planned to call her in a couple of days. She felt satisfied after her first day in her new job. She had instinctively warmed to Florence and was confident they would work well together, possibly become friends, and she hoped she would get on well with Aaron. Antonia was really happy about her decision to leave the airline and move to the tourism industry. She was tired now, though: the two daiquiris had taken effect and it was time to put the papers away and sleep.

TWO

Antonia decided on a light breakfast of orange juice, toast and milky coffee. She had more than an hour until she was due at the office and her thoughts drifted back to her last flight as a cabin crew supervisor.

She couldn't deny that she'd been anxious. She was starting a new life, in a new country, doing a new job. She felt it was a bold move, not something that she ever saw herself doing, let alone in her early thirties. Antonia had refused the offer of a glass of champagne; she was still on duty and would be breaching all the flight safety regs if she even sipped one mouthful. There would be time for a drink or two, or perhaps three, when the crew gathered that evening around the hotel pool.

She was delighted that her final destination was Antigua. The Blue Waves Hotel complex sat on a beautiful bay in the north of Antigua and served wonderful food and drinks. The airline had generously offered Antonia two nights at the hotel with the crew during their layover at the firm's expense, even though she was no longer an employee. She was thrilled to buddy up and share a room with one of the new recruits, a petite, copper-haired Scottish girl called Kirsty, who only had two years' crew experience with a regional airline operating from Edinburgh. She was clearly very excited to be on her first Caribbean trip. Antonia could vividly recall her own first long-haul flight, which had been to New York, and instinctively felt proud of young Kirsty, just starting her career as Antonia was closing the chapter on her life with the airline. The crew would be departing in two days on the return flight to Gatwick, then Antonia would move to her rented flat in Jolly Harbour on the west of the island. In the meantime, she could relax and reminisce with her colleagues, and relive their adventures on their US and Caribbean long-haul flights.

To remember her ten years with the company, the crew had given her a lovely pair of pearl earrings and a gorgeous bikini in the bright red of the airline's logo, from a very expensive Paris fashion house.

Antonia smiled as she recalled the saying that always made her click into work mode: 'Cabin crew, prepare for landing'. When they heard this, the crew immediately began to carry out their routine: seats upright, trays up, bags stowed, doors to manual and cross-checked. A quick glance out of a window showed the blue-green sea flashing by, just a couple of hundred feet below. Antonia took her own seat for landing.

The passengers and crew were very glad to get off the plane after the journey they had experienced. A Category 3 hurricane tracking from east to west had buffeted the flight for a solid two hours across the mid-Atlantic, with the winds only relenting as they approached the Caribbean islands. Even experienced flyers disliked the sudden drops, the surges of power as the pilot worked hard to keep the aircraft on course, and the thought of a heavy, possibly disastrous, landing. Those of a nervous disposition held their fingers against their temples; some held the armrests with a vice-like grip and stared forlornly ahead; couples were holding hands; some nonchalant or carefree travellers kept their cheerful demeanour through it all.

Antonia had long ago lost any apprehension about flying in rough weather and she was delighted to see Kirsty take it in her stride: those inter-island flights in the Hebrides and Orkneys must have prepared her for all conditions.

The approach was skilfully executed with hardly a bump on touchdown. In the few minutes it took to taxi to the airbridge, Antonia closed her eyes for a moment and smiled to herself, realising that this was it: the start of a completely new life on her favourite island in the sun.

Her watch chimed an alarm and Antonia realised that her daydreaming was in danger of making her late. She cleared away her breakfast things, gathered her work papers together and focused on the day ahead.

THREE

Even eighteen months into the job, Peter knew he would never grow tired of his daily early morning walk along Ffryes beach. Around five feet ten inches tall, he kept himself slim and supple with a range of exercises every day. His naturally fair hair was made lighter by the sun, but he was careful about too much exposure and had only a light suntan.

The lapping waves and the warmth of the sun lifted his energy and gave him an appetite for his regular Caribbean breakfast: mango juice, sliced papaya and black pineapple with a bowl of muesli and a black coffee. He didn't mind being a creature of habit; he liked to have a routine and know what the day had in store for him.

He'd only returned from the UK the day before, following his second trip home since arriving on the island, and now he was back he wanted to swim. To feel the caressing warmth of the Caribbean Sea was a pleasure he always enjoyed, made all the more sensual by the rhythmic rising and falling of the waves. He usually took a snorkel and mask, as he loved to see the array of fish and plant life that lived around the rocks at the far end of the bay, but today he knew the water would be too cloudy. The hurricane might have been a hundred miles away, but its strong winds had stirred up the waves and sand to create a fog of sparkling particles that would spoil the normally crystal-clear waters for three or four days.

The swim left him invigorated and he ran the half mile home to his small, modern, two-bedroomed house in a terrace of six, set back from the beach. The company owned the houses and let them to senior employees who didn't mind living 'above the shop' – a modern water treatment plant. The heat even at seven thirty in the morning was stifling and only a cold shower could reduce his body temperature enough so that he could dress. As he sat at the tiny breakfast table in the kitchenette, he rummaged through the papers and spreadsheets that had been delivered to his flat the day before by George Robartes, the chief scientist at the Dart Water Health Company – or DWH, as it was known locally.

Peter admired Robartes: he was an Antiguan success story. At the age of eleven, he had been sent to stay with an uncle in England, having passed the selection tests to attend a grammar school. He did marvellously well and applied for a place at the University of Oxford. He had the good fortune to have a distant cousin who worked for the Antigua Civil Service, who spoke to the university on George's behalf, and George was awarded one of the scholarships handed out as part of Antigua's celebrations of its independence, which was granted in 1981. George shone at Oxford, gaining a first-class honours degree in chemistry. Now, with only months left until George's retirement, Peter was hopeful, or, perhaps expecting, that he would take over George's job at the plant. He was immensely satisfied with his decision to leave the UK and work abroad. After three years in Australia working on groundwater extraction projects, he had seen an advert for the position of head of engineering with DWH in Antigua. He applied straight away and, after three online assessments, was invited to the island for a final interview with the plant directors and government representatives. Peter passed the assessments with flying colours and had no hesitation in accepting the job, both for his career progression and because he wanted a fresh start after a traumatic relationship break-up – and he felt that the culture and atmosphere of Antigua were right for him. He liked the lifestyle Antigua offered and, after the first couple of months, he knew he fitted well into island life.

But he wasn't the sort of person who was obsessed by work; he liked to balance his interests in sport and music with his role behind a desk or in a testing lab. He tuned his smart speakers to radio stations around the world to pick up jazz and country music from the US, world affairs from the BBC, and Caribbean news and sounds from local stations. As well as swimming and running, he liked to go to the gym and occasionally played for the water company's cricket team. He joined the prestigious Cedar Hills Golf Club and played most Sunday mornings with a friendly group of local residents – Antiguan and expat. He felt he had a good life in Antigua and was committed to seeking permanent residency as soon as he could.

If he had one uncertainty about the lifestyle, it was about future relationships. Would he meet a partner here? However, he was philosophical about it, he didn't want to go out looking for a partner, and he hated the idea of online dating or singles clubs. Some of the guys at the plant had encouraged him to socialise with them at bars in St John's and English Harbour, and they had introduced him to plenty of lovely local and expat women. He knew he could have developed a rapport with any one of half a dozen ladies, but held back from getting into casual relationships. If he met a girl he really felt something for, great, but he wanted it to happen naturally. His priority was his work. He wanted to do well at DWH and get the promotion to the chief scientist job.

FOUR

After spending the first week largely in the office, Antonia decided she needed to get out and explore the island on her own. She had been introduced to Corinne Scott, the owner of Jolly Harbour Auto Rentals, one evening in the Mango Tree and Corinne had offered her a seriously discounted rate for a long-term car rental. Antonia took up Corinne's offer and, with a free weekend ahead of her, spread out a map and planned her tour.

She felt she had been given a good introduction to the capital, St John's, and the cruise ship terminal and visitor centre. It was time to head south, so she decided on a drive to the bay at Falmouth for a late breakfast and then further round to the historical fortress of English Harbour. The range of restaurants there amazed Antonia and she enjoyed the hustle and bustle of yacht owners and crew around the harbour. It made her feel excited about her job. It was going to be so stimulating and enjoyable, as there were always going to be avenues to explore to generate more tourism for the island.

Partly for her own interest and partly as she wanted to improve her knowledge of the history of Antigua for her job, Antonia spent an hour in the Nelson's Dockyard district. She found the Georgian dry dock, the remnants of the sail loft and the officers' quarters fascinating and strangely atmospheric. They evoked mental pictures of Jack Tars in blue and white uniforms and naval officers stifling in serge jackets and bicorn hats. She took in the museum after lunch, avoiding being outside in the mid-afternoon heat. Ideas for cultural tours started to form in her mind – she knew that Antigua was not just about beaches and sailing, but she hadn't realised how much history it had. She concluded there were some terrific attractions for history buffs and decided to find out which tours were currently available, and how these were promoted by the Ministry of Tourism.

Returning to her car in the late afternoon, Antonia decided to take a slow drive back home. The road climbed through the dense greenery of the central hills for about five miles, before turning down to the west coast. As she drove through the small villages, she saw that not everyone on Antigua had money; in fact, some of the houses were virtually shanties. People sat in small groups on front porches, some had rickety stalls selling fruit and vegetables. She kept her eyes on the road ahead – there were treacherous potholes and broken roadsides to negotiate. She suddenly saw a more organised row of stalls, so she pulled over.

Walking along the beautiful displays of fruit, herbs, salads, peppers and other vegetables, she noted that no prices were shown. Antonia smiled to herself. She knew that there were prices for locals and very much higher prices for tourists and expats. She didn't care and was inwardly pleased that her purchase of a large bag of fruit would help to support the people of the island.

Back in the car, she headed north again. The condition of the road improved as she approached the Carillion Bay resort. Florence had mentioned the hotel as being one of the most luxurious on the island and Antonia had a meeting with the senior management team in her diary for the following week. Antonia slowed and peered through the bougainvillea hedge at the immaculate hotel buildings. She then passed several more beautiful bays, all of which had hotels and restaurants capitalising on their beach position and the wonderful views. She pulled over when she arrived at Darkwood beach, parked and got out of the car. She breathed in deeply, taking pleasure in the scent of the trees and the freshness of the sea air. She decided that she would return another day to swim in the bay.

After another few minutes of driving, Antonia saw the grass sunshades lining Ffryes beach, gently swaying in the breeze. The bay was almost deserted, so she parked the car, took off her shoes and walked across the fine silver-yellow sand to the water's edge. The sun was almost down to the horizon and across the aquamarine sea were streaks of golden light – the beginning of a classic Caribbean sunset. Although she knew it would quickly get dark after the sun disappeared, she decided to stay and watch the spectacle.

The warm, shallow water was so soothing and the waves seemed to work in perfect harmony with the breeze. As the sun sank below the horizon, she noticed an island in the distance; she had to shield her eyes as the pink and gold rays cast upwards to the sky and the distant island became a mesmerising silhouette. Then, in only a couple of minutes, the sun disappeared and a deep twilight fell. The few clouds high in the sky lost their red edging and turned grey. It was time to go.

As Antonia turned around to leave, she was startled to see someone standing no more than ten yards behind her – a man in bright blue shorts and a white T-shirt with an Antiguan flag logo.

"It's Montserrat," he said.

Antonia was too stunned to think straight. "What?" was all she could manage to say.

"The island you were looking at. It's Montserrat."

"Oh, right, is it?"

"Hey, I'm sorry, didn't mean to creep up on you like that. I often come to this beach on evenings when the sunset is likely to be dazzling. Pretty impressive, wasn't it?"

"Yes, it certainly was."

"Hang on a minute – I think I know you." The man took a few steps forward.

Antonia was immediately suspicious. It was a line she had heard before from men trying it on. How the hell could he know her? She had only been on the island a few days. "I don't think so," she said firmly.

"I remember – you were on the Gatwick flight last week. You were cabin crew – I was on that flight! Hell of a lumpy crossing, wasn't it? Fortunately, the hurricane was played out and heading away from the Caribbean. There will be more, though; we're in the season now and they tend to come along one after another. Something was going on, was it your birthday, perhaps? I'm afraid I didn't take much notice of the celebrations, I was watching the end of a film."

Antonia visibly relaxed. "Yes, that was me – not a birthday, but my last flight with the airline. I've taken a job here on the island with the Ministry of Tourism. The guys gave me a lovely send-off."

"Excellent, so you live here now?"

"Yes, but I'm still finding my way around. I drove over to English Harbour this afternoon and stopped off here on my way back to Jolly Harbour to enjoy the view. How about you? Are you on holiday?"

"No, I live here, too. A little way inland is where I work – and past there are the workers' huts where I live."

"Huts?" Antonia smiled at the man. She knew he was kidding her.

"Well, a nice little house, actually, provided by the firm, so I guess I'm quite lucky."

The sky was almost dark, but a half-moon and myriad stars shone so brightly that Antonia and the man could clearly see each other.

Spontaneously, they started to walk slowly along the water's edge. Small waves occasionally washed over Antonia's feet.

"And what do you do, work-wise?" asked Antonia.

"I'm an engineer with the Antiguan water company. About half a mile behind those trees is the RO plant."

Antonia looked puzzled.

"Sorry – 'reverse osmosis'. We take seawater and filter it, so it's ready for drinking, cooking, washing and so on. The big challenge is designing a process that is cost-effective and produces enough water to make it all worthwhile. Antigua has very little natural fresh water."

"Can you drink the tap water here? I've only seen people drink from bottles."

"That's probably wise if you're not used to the local water. I recommend staying with bottled water – that's not much of an advert for what we do, I'm afraid."

They laughed gently. They had come to the end of the beach and a rocky cliff face stretched above them.

"You see those lights up there? That's Diana's bar. Can I buy you a drink?" Peter asked.

The bar was on the first level of the raised headland and had tables laid out under a large wooden canopy. *The view must be magnificent*, Antonia thought. She was pleased that she'd met this man, but this was all too sudden. She wasn't the sort of woman to be picked up on a beach.

"That's kind of you, but perhaps another time. Have a good evening." Antonia turned and started to walk purposefully back to her car.

He called out to her. "I shall look forward to it! What's your name?"

She stopped and turned. "Antonia."

"Pleased to meet you, Antonia. I'm Peter. Peter Devon."

FIVE

On the drive back to Jolly Harbour, Antonia couldn't stop smiling to herself. Peter seemed a lovely man and she half-wished she had accepted his offer of a drink. She had no idea if their paths would ever cross again, but she couldn't deny that she hoped they would.

It was two years since she'd separated from Steve. He had betrayed her; after they'd lived together for over six years, he had begun a relationship with a new colleague at the bank where he worked. It had been easy for him, with her regular long-haul flights keeping her away from home. Within three weeks of meeting the woman, he'd left. Although Antonia had been hurt at the time, she now regarded their relationship as a thing of the past and was revelling in her new-found freedom and independence. She had dated a few men, without feeling any real connection with them, but now wasn't the time to become involved with another man. That wasn't what she had come to the island for.

Just as she arrived back at the apartment block, she congratulated herself on declining Peter's invitation. She was a self-assured woman with a clear life plan.

***

On her second Monday, Antonia spent the day with Aaron, exchanging views on the prospects for developing new and existing sources of tourists. Room occupancy data and flight arrivals for the past two years, since the Covid crisis, showed clear peaks and significant troughs. Fortunately, the cruise industry had recovered well after the pandemic, with the largest ships now scheduling St John's as a regular stop on the Caribbean circuit. The question was: how could the tourism industry on the island offer the best experience to passengers who only had one day in port?

Not surprisingly, visitors stayed away during the hurricane season, which was generally regarded as being July to November – almost half the year. It meant that December to June was the peak season when the tourism industry needed to make money. This was when so many people from the UK and US wanted to travel to escape the winter weather, so it was no surprise that this was the busiest time of the year. Antonia had arrived in June, so had missed the height of the season, as well as the big sailing events – Antigua Sailing Week and the Antigua Regatta for Oyster owners. This didn't concern her, as it would give her time to research and plan activities for the following season, assuming that Aaron approved her plans.

She was particularly keen to discuss ideas for historical and cultural holidays, while acknowledging that beach holidays would always be the biggest attraction for visitors. The dockyard museum in English Harbour had fed her interest in the emancipation of slaves on the island and the wider Caribbean and US, but she was not sure whether the story of slavery and sugar plantations would readily interest visitors, even in the context of the history of the region. But, she decided she must, at least, start the discussion.

SIX

Even though she enjoyed her work, Antonia looked forward to the weekend and her free time. She was determined to continue her exploration of Antigua. This Saturday she was heading away from the beaches. She joined a walking tour of Mount Obama, the highest point on the island, guided by a local man in his sixties called Marley who seemed to know the name of every plant, flower, bird and insect. Marley explained that the mountain had been nicknamed 'Boggy Peak' back in the days of slavery, but had been formally renamed to honour the achievements of a black man in becoming President of the United States. The climb was more demanding than Antonia had expected and she was glad she was wearing her trainers. But it was worth the effort, as the view from the top of the peak was stunning. Way over to the north, she could see the white buildings and yachts at Jolly Harbour; to her left was Darkwood beach; and straight ahead was Ffryes beach and the headland, where she could just see a white-roofed building that must be Diana's – the bar and restaurant that Peter had pointed out.

It was a fascinating day and it gave her lots of ideas to attract tourists interested in ecology, as well as those who liked to learn about the social and economic history of places they visited. After the tour, she drove the short distance to Ffryes beach and parked the car. She had time to spare and decided to get a drink at Diana's. It was mid-afternoon on a Saturday, the changeover day for tourists, so there were few people in the bar and she didn't feel at all self-conscious about being on her own.

She took a table close to the front of the shaded veranda and looked out at the beautiful smooth sand of the bay, which curved away into the distance. At the far end of the beach, another land mass grew out of the sea, larger than the small promontory where Diana had built her bar. Antonia had seen the signposts and gated entrance telling the world that Tamarind Hills was private property. She could see the white villas and apartments on the hill, all designed to give the most stunning views across the turquoise Caribbean Sea.

The people on the beach were almost entirely local families, swimming, sunbathing and eating the picnics they had brought with them. A lively breeze came onshore from the west. There were more clouds today, towering cotton-wool cumulus ones, white-topped, some with an ominous grey mass in the centre. A heavy rain shower was approaching.

As her drink was brought to her table, the wind strengthened and a few drops of rain, the size of marbles, splashed onto the lower terrace. Within minutes, a cacophonous downpour rattled the roof of the bar and sent the people on the beach running to the shelter of the grass sunshades. Antonia spontaneously laughed – not at the predicament of the beach families, but at the sheer pleasure she found in witnessing a feature of Caribbean life. The showers were as welcome as the unbroken sunny days. But the storm was over quickly, the sun soon cut through the clouds and the people returned, led by excited children, who ran down to the sea's edge.

Antonia savoured her mango, orange and coconut mocktail, listening to the lively Caribbean music coming from a CD player. She glanced around at the few other guests in the bar. People-watching was a favourite pastime of hers. A group of holidaymakers were becoming more vocal as the rum punches were consumed. At least some tourists were still coming to the island, taking the risk of their holiday being a washout and being confined to their hotel if a hurricane should come within a hundred miles of the island.

Maybe the couple sitting on stools at the bar, both with deep suntans, were expats at their favourite haunt, chatting with the barman as regular clients would. The man was probably in his mid-sixties: short silver hair, not overweight but not slim, fit-looking. He had the confidence to wear a bright tropical shirt illustrated with palm trees over a deep pink background. He wore beach shoes, on which Antonia could just see the Hermès logo. The lady was younger, petite and clearly also looked after herself. She wore shorts and a matching cream linen shirt that Antonia thought looked perfect for the heat. Expensive-looking designer sunglasses perched on top of her well-groomed dark brown hair. They had the dress style of the international set – they would look good anywhere in the world. Diana spent some time chatting to them; Antonia heard snatches of discussion about the West Indies cricket team and the best places to eat in English Harbour.

Antonia checked the time on her watch. It was just past five thirty; an hour earlier than the time she'd been at Ffryes when she'd met Peter. She decided to finish her drink and not wait to see the sunset. She admitted to herself that she was disappointed Peter wasn't there and felt a loss of self-control at the pull of her emotions and her attraction to the man. It had been a foolish hope that she might bump into him and she was annoyed with herself that thoughts of meeting Peter had driven her to call into the bar. She vowed not to do it again.

SEVEN

The St John's cruise terminal was eerily quiet as Antonia and Florence walked from the car park through the tourist shopping district. They were on their way to the port authority offices to meet members of their management team. Although some cruise ships continued to operate in the Caribbean throughout the year, most operators took their ships to other destinations at the height of the hurricane season. At times in the summer, the terminal could be empty. Now, in late July, there was one ship in dock; its passengers were all on shore trips. Not one of the mega cruise ships was expected in the coming month.

Florence pointed out some of her favourite shops in the port area and around Heritage Quay, a quaint but smart historical district now home to an array of high-end shops, bars and restaurants. They were all fully stocked, ready for the surge in trade that was expected in the autumn.

At the port offices, after introductions were made, Antonia talked about her ideas for beach-based, cultural and historical tourism and how these would fit into the cruise ships' calendar. The port authority only really had one focus: to make day or overnight passengers' visits as fruitful as possible for island businesses. Very few cruises actually started or finished in Antigua, so it was critical that day visitors were treated to the best experience possible in entertainment, local interest and shopping opportunities. If the tourism industry could provide the best of all these attractions, then the cruise ships would keep coming and St John's would feature as one of the Caribbean's must-visit destinations on their itineraries. Cruise ships all paid port fees, which supported the island's economy.

She had seen it for herself on previous visits to St John's: as cruise ship passengers disembarked, they were whisked away in taxis or twelve-seater buses on pre-booked tours, or were persuaded by smooth-talking sales reps to take a trip to the main places of interest. Destinations were predictable; Falmouth and English Harbour, Shirley Heights Lookout, a walking tour of the Sir Vivian Richards Stadium for cricket lovers, various restaurants specialising in Caribbean food and, of course, the main beaches around the island. Shopping at duty-free outlets was always a priority for passengers and the best shops faced the terminal: they were the first and last thing passengers would see on their visit.

Antonia asked about interest in the island's history, back to when sugar was the dominant crop and brought wealth to the island. She sensed that the port staff, as well as many others she had met from various government departments, didn't warm to her ideas about guided tours of slavery-related sites. She felt that the people she was meeting in the tourism industry welcomed her with open arms and universally seemed excited at her ideas for planning new tourist experiences, but a pattern was developing. They all seemed reluctant to discuss matters related to the slavery period of their history. She decided to put her ideas on the back burner. She was the new girl on the block, after all, and she didn't want to upset anyone.

After their meeting at the port offices, Florence asked Antonia if she would like to have lunch at a restaurant popular with locals and tourists – Harriett's. They sat on the first-floor veranda, taking in the views across the busy street. It reminded Antonia of the French quarter in New Orleans and she had to tell herself to concentrate on talking to Florence, rather than watching the passers-by below. She tilted her hat to provide shade against the brightness and heat of the sun, and so that she could clearly see Florence.

"What do you think, Florence… are people not keen to develop tourism based on Antigua's history of slavery? When you look at the thousands of visitors who come through the port, surely many of them want to see more of the island's history? After all, when you visit places like Barcelona, Athens or Havana, people are attracted by the history, aren't they? I don't want to tread on any toes or be clumsy and appear insensitive. Is it pointless thinking about it?"

Florence sat back, pursed her lips and twitched her nose in thoughtful mode. "Not exactly. Sure, the slave trade background is a hated part of the island's history, but there are various places where cultural tourists are welcomed. You've been to the dockyard museum… and then there's Betty's Hope. Have you visited there yet?"

"No, what is it?"

"It's an old sugar plantation. There are two windmills. One has been renovated; the other is derelict. There are also other buildings on the site and artefacts from the time. It's all very well done. You might have seen some old, dilapidated windmills around the island; there are more than a hundred of them, with many hidden under decades of ivy and weeds. The mills were used to crush the sugar cane and extract the juice. This was then boiled to produce sugar. Incredibly hard work – and dangerous. Many Antiguans are concerned about the commercialisation of that part of our history."

"I can understand that," said Antonia. "Seems that a sensitive touch is required, or perhaps I should avoid it entirely?"

Florence sat up and put on her best smile. "Don't let me put you off! If you have good ideas on how we can offer interesting and relevant historical tourism based on our emancipation from slavery, that would be very welcome, I'm sure. But there should be no hint of hopelessness for the black people from those times. Terrible though slavery was, the freedom that was obtained is to be celebrated."

"So the first thing I should do is visit Betty's Hope and learn more about the history of sugar production and slavery, as well as how emancipation was achieved?"

"Yes, and I will come with you. This afternoon, I will call Jacetta Whitworth, who's the manager there, and arrange a date for our visit. Jacetta will give us a proper tour and a look through the artefacts and document archives she keeps. I'm sure you will find it hugely interesting."

"That would be brilliant, Florence. Thank you so much."

"You're welcome. Now, one more thing…" Florence took on a serious tone.

"Yes?"

"Lunch. Let me recommend the lobster salad – it's wonderful here!"

EIGHT

There was clearly something wrong when Antonia arrived for work on a hot, blustery Monday morning in mid-August. Florence and Aaron were huddled over a computer screen and Antonia only received a quick 'good morning', rather than the more expansive greeting she was used to. Florence had a notepad open and a pencil in her hand. Antonia quickly hung up her jacket and walked over to Florence's desk.

"Category 3 by Wednesday, increasing to 4 on Thursday," said Aaron. "Tracking across the eastern Caribbean to the north of the Turks and Caicos towards the Bahamas. Looks like we're going to get hit pretty hard later in the week." He glanced up. "Hi, Antonia, have a look at this. We're in for some bad weather. Hurricane Lorna is brewing out in the Atlantic and is headed our way. Watch this simulation." Aaron clicked the mouse and the map of the Caribbean and the west of the Atlantic Ocean came to life as a circle of arrows moved in unison to show the predicted position of the hurricane every six hours, travelling from east to west, curving upwards and away from Antigua by Thursday.

"Those islands in the north are going to get hit full on, but fortunately we should avoid the strongest winds and highest seas."

"Category 4 – sounds nasty," said Antonia.

Florence stood back from the screen. "It sure is. We're likely to see a lot of property damage, the sea will be churned up and there'll be a hell of a lot of rain. All the hotels, restaurants and other businesses will lock down, probably from Wednesday through to Saturday – maybe longer if the hurricane changes direction and comes closer to us."

"And I'll be closing the office from tonight," said Aaron. "You should stay indoors, Antonia, and stay safe. I will call staff to let everyone know when we will reopen, but let's plan for Saturday morning, if you don't mind coming into the office at the weekend?"

"No, not at all," Antonia replied, realising that she would have to postpone her plans.

"And make sure you have plenty of food and water at home. I recommend you get along to the Gourmand supermarket this morning if you need anything," said Florence.

"Thanks, I will do that. I have some food and drinks at home, of course, but I'll need more to get me through three or four days."

"OK, but make it a week of supplies. You should go now. There will be a big rush when people see the forecast. Remember to buy plenty of water – and forget frozen food. There may well be power cuts."

"Right. Is it OK if I go now, Aaron?" Antonia asked.

"For sure. Get everything you need and take a taxi home. We'll see you back here around lunchtime."

***

As predicted, there was a queue at the main door of the Gourmand. Inside, it was full and the aisles were bustling with customers keen to buy all they needed. Antonia felt the sense of urgency and purpose that seemed to unite everyone: they were all facing the same danger. She spent time carefully choosing necessaries like pasta, rice, bread, vegetables, tins of meat and fish, cartons of fruit juice, long-life milk and two cases of bottled water. Satisfied that she had all the supplies she'd require for a week of lockdown and post-hurricane shortages, she turned her shopping trolley towards one of the tills. The queue was slow-moving, since every customer had a large pile of goods. As she stood waiting patiently, Antonia's thoughts started to wander to where she might like to explore after the hurricane and she gazed idly around the shop.

And then she saw him. A couple of places ahead of her in the next queue, on the other side of a high rack displaying tempting snacks and chocolate bars. Peter was facing forward and wouldn't see her unless he turned around. He was on his own and was obviously stocking up, the same as her. She almost called out, but then what? How could they talk across the crowd? What on earth could she say? Her frustration grew as he stoically waited, watching the people ahead. She willed with all her concentration that he would turn around.

But nothing happened. When he reached the till he simply loaded his shopping onto the counter, the assistant packed up his purchases and he paid the bill. Without looking round, he pushed his trolley out to the car park. Like their encounter at Ffryes beach, she felt the sensation of a lost opportunity. She could have called out to him or dashed after him. Her reluctance to seize the moment had led to her feeling disappointed. It was becoming the story of her life; she seemed to watch the world like a spectator. Little excitement came her way; she felt dull, invisible. Absent-mindedly, she completed her shopping and joined a queue of people standing in the shade to wait for a taxi.

Two elderly women in front of her were talking about the coming hurricane, debating whether it was likely to be more devastating than Irma or last longer than Luis. She was mesmerised by their stories of how villages in the interior of the island had been smashed to pieces, how seawater had come a mile inland in places, how food and water supplies had run out. But then Antonia smiled to herself, as she realised the women were trying to out-scare each other with tales of the destruction they had lived through. A taxi had taken the first person in the queue and soon another arrived. After a few moments, another taxi came and off went the first elderly lady. To Antonia's anguish, the remaining lady had not finished her story and felt the need to regale Antonia with her recollections. Antonia nodded politely and simply said, 'Gosh,' at the right time to all the catastrophic events the lady had witnessed.

Then, a car horn sounded. They both looked over.

It was a white Mazda SUV. The driver's window was open and a voice called out. "Hi, Antonia! Can I give you a lift?"

It took Antonia a moment to register that the man in the car, wearing sunglasses, was Peter.

NINE

She was hugely grateful for Peter's help to carry all her shopping up to her flat on the first floor. In the short drive from the supermarket, the pair only talked about the hurricane and the damage it would cause. They took the bags of food and cases of water through to the kitchen.

Antonia checked the time. She had about an hour until she was due back at the office; any later would be taking liberties with Aaron's kindness in giving her the morning off to do her shopping. However, she didn't want Peter to leave straight away.

"Thanks, Peter, that was very kind of you. Can I get you a drink? Orange juice or coffee, perhaps?"

"Well, yes, coffee would be great, thank you."

Antonia sensed he felt uncertain. "Are you sure? Do you have time?"

Peter's shoulders relaxed and he held up his hands. Smiling, he said, "It won't hurt if I'm out of the office a little longer. Coffee would indeed be great, thank you."

They took their drinks through to the living room and sat at the small dining table. Antonia nodded towards the picture window, which framed the view of the harbour and the sea beyond. "Those clouds look ominous and the wind is getting stronger. Have there been any big storms since you arrived?"

"No. Apparently there was a nasty one a couple of years ago, but nothing as big as Hurricane Lorna is expected to be."

"Sounds like it's going to be quite a show. Frightening, really."

"Yes, the noise will be deafening and the wind will shake the buildings. You know you shouldn't go out during a hurricane? It would be very dangerous – flying debris, trees, even small boats can be lifted into the air." Peter stood and went to the window. "No rain yet, but it will be hellish when it comes."

Antonia had her first chance to look at him properly. She was taller than average herself, but comfortably within the height accepted as cabin crew. Peter was marginally taller, fit and slim and with lovely fair hair, cut short. She had already registered his blue eyes and wide smile.

"Will you have to be at work during the hurricane, keeping the water flowing?" asked Antonia.

"No, the plant will be locked down tomorrow. Like everyone else, I will spend a couple of days at home, hoping for the best. The worst of it should be over by Saturday."

"That would be good. My boss is planning to reopen the office Saturday morning."

"I'll bet there will be a lot of damaged boats out there. The local reps from insurance companies will be busy handling claims and it will be a boom time for boatyards doing repairs." He looked at his watch. "I'd better be going, Antonia. Thanks for the coffee."

"My pleasure. Maybe we could have that drink after all the excitement has died down?"

Antonia blushed as she realised she had taken the initiative. He had done her a simple favour with the lift home and might feel under pressure to accept, even though he had asked the same of her on Ffryes beach. She need not have worried.

"That would be brilliant. Why don't I give you a call on Sunday, assuming that the phones are working?"

"Sure, that would work. Here's my card. It has my mobile number on it, as well as the office."

Peter took out his wallet and found a card of his own. She walked Peter to the door. As he stepped out onto the balcony, he turned around and said, "Best of luck over the week ahead. Take care." He gave her arm a gentle squeeze.

"You, too. Bye for now."

She closed the door and took a deep breath. *Bloody hell*, she thought. *That was a surprise.* She already knew she wanted to see Peter again and that meant she risked stirring up her emotions. If he didn't feel the same, she would be hurt. She had enjoyed his company, why deny that? She'd just see where it went; there was nothing wrong with having a drink together, she assured herself.

***

Less than an hour later, she was back in the office. Aaron was on the phone to the met office in St John's and Florence was at her computer, compiling a news briefing. It was important that communications with the outside world were carefully managed. The media were likely to sensationalise the storm, seeking to gain readers and keep their advertisers happy. The Ministry of Tourism would report the facts. If there was a positive slant to be found, then they would find it and ensure the travel industry and potential tourists got to hear about it.

The phone rang. Florence asked Antonia to take the call. She answered – she was glad to help and wanted to feel she had a role to play. It was the Sugar Hills development. They wanted the ministry to repost details of the contingency arrangements for guests who could not get flights home due to the hurricane on their website. Antonia had seen the beautiful villas at Sugar Hills on the hill overlooking Jolly Harbour. They generously offered up to four days' additional accommodation at no extra charge. Good PR and, of course, the guests would spend more money in the bar and restaurant. Then, Antonia took a call from the port authority, giving an update on the shipping movements planned for the day; essentially a list of ships heading south in a hurry, away from the hurricane's course.

By the end of the afternoon, all the arrangements were in place for the coming week. Aaron had told the team they should come into the office in the morning if the weather wasn't too bad to update the website, if necessary, and take any calls for advice. After that, the staff could work from home, for as long as their internet connections held up. Aaron said he would monitor progress of the hurricane on the storm tracker website and liaise with the major tourist centres and government departments. Antonia was impressed by Aaron and the speed at which he took action; he was a diligent manager and an assured decision-maker.

It was now a case of waiting to see what Lorna would bring to the islands.

TEN

At just after five on Tuesday morning, Antonia woke with a start; roof tiles crashing to the ground from a building in the harbour spoke of the arrival of Hurricane Lorna. Antonia had been vaguely conscious of hearing a car alarm go off during the night and now the booming sound of the strengthening wind would prevent any further sleep.

After checking she still had power, she made coffee and switched on her computer, glad to find that the internet was still up. The hurricane tracking site showed that the centre of Lorna had moved west and was now to the north of the island, almost exactly as predicted. Over the next two days, the hurricane would move away to the north-west and, crucially, the winds in the Antigua region would weaken to be a tropical storm by Thursday.

***

At first light, Antonia drew back the blinds on her window. The row of palm trees in the road below were bent at a 45-degree angle and were being shaken crazily by the wind. Two or three trees were missing, having been uprooted completely. Pieces of timber flashed through the air, torn away from fencing and buildings. And, most worrying of all, waves were crashing over the boardwalk and against the buildings along the harbour.

She felt fear run through her as she wondered if her apartment building would be strong enough to withstand the wind, which was pounding the building like a series of heavyweight punches. Suddenly, a piece of wood – it looked like a section of picket fencing from the golf club – struck the window, making her jump backwards. A crack had formed at one corner of the window, but the glass had held. She had seen the warnings not to stand too close to windows and now she understood why. Antonia wondered about the houses she had seen in the villages along the road to English Harbour. How could those wooden buildings survive intact? What was happening to the people inside?

As the morning progressed, the low clouds tumbled westwards and a heavy rain fell. The sky's colours of grey, green and white swirled and merged, and the atmosphere was oppressively humid. All day the wind hammered the building and Antonia sat anxiously at her desk, expecting the roof to be ripped off at any moment. She couldn't concentrate on work. The power remained on, but as she prepared to cook an evening meal, she found that the mains water had been cut off and realised how vital it was to have a bottled supply. She used the minimum required to cook her food, not knowing when the water would be switched back on.

The night saw no respite. The howling wind, vicious rainfall and the increasing amounts of debris flying past got to Antonia. She had kept her fears under control during the day, but now she was unnerved, frightened that a window could break and the storm would blast through her flat, with flying glass cutting her to pieces. Sleep only came in the early hours as exhaustion took over.

***

The forecast for Wednesday morning showed a reduction in wind speed as Lorna careered away towards the Bahamas – but the devastation continued. A line of eight yachts on the hard standing had been ripped from their tie-downs and had toppled over, like a line of dominoes. Sometimes, even the best protective measures were not enough to avoid damage.

In the afternoon, Antonia's mobile phone rang. It was Florence, calling to check on her. *Nice touch*, Antonia thought. She was glad to report that she was in good shape, even if she didn't feel it. Florence said that the only problem she had heard about was with one of the marketing team, who lived with her parents in the hills below Mount Obama. Their house, a modern, solidly built bungalow, had lost its roof and the family had had to be evacuated to a neighbour's house. "No one was injured," Florence said, then finished the call with a request that Antonia phone the next morning for an update on when the office might be reopening.

***

After the third night of strong winds, which were now coming from the north, the wind speed had notably reduced and the rain was intermittent and light, rather than torrential. Antonia could barely see out of her windows as the sea spray had left a thick deposit of salt over them. Wearing a waterproof jacket, she dared to open her front door and stepped out onto the balcony for a better view of the Jolly Harbour complex.

She was stunned by what she saw. There were leaves and branches everywhere, and even some whole palm trees. Pieces of splintered wood and rubbish were strewn across the walkways and gardens. A group of local people were clearing up the smaller items of debris. She went back into her flat to call the office.

The progress of the storm to the west was better than expected and Aaron felt it was safe for staff to travel to the office the next day, Friday. It would be a dress-down day and their main job would be to ensure that the office was ready for formally reopening on Saturday. This gave Antonia the whole of Thursday free, so she found some rubber gloves, changed into trousers and trainers, and tied her hair back. She was ready to go down to help her neighbours deal with the aftermath of the storm. After more than two days locked indoors, she relished a chance to do something positive.

As Antonia stepped out of the door, she heard her phone ringing again, tucked away in her jacket pocket. She thought it would be Florence with another update, so she intended to ignore the call and listen to any message later, but then she turned back to answer it.

"Hello?"

"Hi, Antonia, it's Peter."

She quickly went back into the living room and sat down, in a state of delight and surprise. "Oh, hello, Peter. Is everything OK with you?"

"Yes, all fine. I couldn't wait until Sunday to call, so I thought I'd ring to see how you managed during the hurricane."

"Pretty well, I think. It was frightening at times. I thought something would come crashing through the windows. Fortunately, everything held together."

"Yes, the noise was incredible, wasn't it? The sea from Ffryes beach came right across the road and through the gardens, but fortunately the water was only a few inches deep by the time it reached my house. I'll be drying things out today."

"There are people down at the harbour clearing up and I'm going down to help them. But perhaps I could drive over and help you…?"

"Oh, no, don't do that. It's still dangerous on the roads. And take care if you go out; there will be glass and splintered wood everywhere."

"I will, thanks."

A silence fell, as neither of them wanted to end the call, but Antonia felt she should make the next move. "Could you call me again on Sunday, as we planned? You never know, we might even be able to meet up." She screwed her eyes closed as she waited for a response.

"I will and it would be great to meet. I'll look forward to it. Take care now."

"And you. Thanks for calling."

Antonia went and sat at her table for a few minutes, both to give her heart rate some time to settle and for the broad smile on her face to dissipate. She felt warmed by a glow of happiness that she hadn't felt for a long time – perhaps she never had. She had to take a deep breath when she realised she was experiencing those familiar butterflies in her stomach. And she'd already had that falling feeling – those out-of-self emotions that came with a new relationship. But her excitement had an edge of danger and she now had to manage the fear that Peter might not feel quite the same way as she did.

ELEVEN

True to his word, Peter phoned on Sunday morning. After checking that all was well with Antonia, he suggested that they meet as the weather had improved so much. He offered to come and pick her up, as the roads were still strewn with branches and debris. On his morning walk on Saturday, he had called into Diana's bar and found that Antiguan enterprise was in full swing as the staff had cleared the decking of sand and shells and broken greenery from the palm trees at the back of the beach. The team had even swept away a huge pile of seaweed that had been washed up into the bar. A blackboard had been put on the entrance path, announcing:

Reopening Sunday
Book A Table For Lunch

As Antonia sat down with Peter, Diana brought over the menu and drinks list. Only a limited range of options were available. They both chose mushroom risotto, with pineapple and mango drinks.

The temperature had fallen from the highs during the week and the humidity had faded. It was now beautifully warm and the wind, which only days before had been deadly and destructive, was a refreshingly welcome breeze. Some huge nimbus clouds could be seen in the distance, but the air was crystal clear. Montserrat was visible, sitting on the sharp horizon.

Peter pointed to a group of men and women carrying debris from the beach to an open-backed truck parked on the road. "Those people cleaning up the beach are local volunteers. They were here yesterday. Diana told me they love coming to the beach at weekends and want to see it in good shape."

"That's brilliant," said Antonia, "but surely they have their own houses to clean and repair after the hurricane?"

"Yes, some will, but it's surprising how quickly repairs can be made to the timber houses many of them live in. They just get out a bucket of nails, hammer away and hey presto!"

"I was worried during the worst of the storm that there would be a lot of injuries as houses were blown down."

"There were some casualties, but there are no reports of any fatalities."

"Well, that's good," said Antonia. "There's a lot of damage at Jolly Harbour, especially to boats. And we lost water for a while, but it's back on now."

"Yes, I gather there was some pollution of the supply, but that was fixed within a day or two."

Antonia looked out again at the people clearing the beach. "Oh, look Peter. That couple at the far end – they're not locals, but it seems they're willing to help with the clean-up. Good for them."

The suntanned couple wore gym clothes and trainers. They each carried a heavy-duty plastic waste sack and wore rubber gloves. They picked up seaweed, broken wood, plastic bottles and pieces of rubbish that had been blown into the sea and were now washed up onto the beach.

"I've seen them here at the bar a few times. I think they live at Tamarind Hills – that's the complex at the far end," said Peter.

"Yes, I saw them when I called into the bar last week…" Antonia hesitated when she realised she had mentioned being at the bar again. But Peter didn't react, so she continued, "I think of them as 'the international couple', always looking immaculate and comfortable with themselves."

Peter smiled. "Yes, I see what you mean. Living the life here in the Caribbean in these beautiful surroundings must be good for the soul."

As the waiter took away their plates and left the dessert menu, Antonia framed a question she had wanted to ask back at her apartment when Peter had helped with her shopping. "Can I ask, is there a significant other in your life?" Antonia knew she had to ask; she had no desire to get close to Peter if he was involved with another woman.

"No," he said. "I was in a relationship back in the UK and we went to work in Australia together – but that was over a long time ago. I have a new life here; I don't think about the past much." Peter gave a short, nervous laugh.

Antonia understood that to mean he didn't want to talk about it and reluctantly didn't ask any further questions. She looked carefully at him for signs of regret or sadness, but there were none: his eyes sparkled and he had laughter lines on his cheeks. And then the inevitable question came. "And how about you? Do you have a dashing airline pilot keen to make his final landing here in Antigua?"

"No, I'm very much single. I had a boyfriend called Steve, but that ended two years ago." Antonia felt pleased that Peter was single; it didn't mean they would jump into a relationship, but it was good to know. Their pasts would influence how they felt about future romances. Perhaps they would both be cautious or even averse to getting together, but Antonia knew she really liked Peter. He was a good-looking man, had a lovely smile and seemed to have a good sense of humour. She wanted to get to know him – slowly and cautiously, if that's what he wanted, too.

They had coffee and Peter paid the bill.

"The next one's on me," said Antonia. "Would you like to take a walk along the beach, now it's been nicely cleaned up by our international couple?"

"Good plan. Let's go down there."

They took their shoes off and walked along the shoreline, ankle-deep in the shallow, foaming water. However, the after effects of the hurricane meant that a few lively waves washed in and they danced away, up the beach, laughing. Antonia realised that Peter had taken her hand. As the water subsided, he didn't let go. She was happy with that and gave his hand a gentle squeeze. They reached the end of the beach and looked up to the villas and apartments. Antonia pointed to a large property on the headland that had the most stunning view of the Caribbean Sea ahead and Ffryes beach below.

"That place must be worth millions," she said.

"All the properties here are expensive – it's one of the most desirable places on the island. Only a few people actually live here; most are holiday lets or occupied for a few weeks or months a year by their owners. Shall we walk back?"

"Sure," said Antonia. "And if you're giving me a lift home, I can make some drinks there, if you have time?"

"I have all the time in the world…" Peter said in a sing-song voice.

They both laughed and Peter slipped his arm around Antonia's waist, holding her gently.

A much larger wave crashed onto the beach, creating a boom and a rush of sand, pebbles and shells as it ran up the shore. They were engulfed in water up to their knees and they held on to each other as the wave subsided, almost dragging them into the sea. When it reached its furthest point out, before the next wave was formed, Antonia spotted something in the sand.

"Peter, did you see that? There was a box or something, buried in the sand."

"No. What did it look like?"

"About the size of a shoebox, rusted metal. Let's wait for the next big wave."

But after ten minutes of watching waves come in and wash out, they hadn't seen the box again. Antonia felt she was holding Peter up and imagined him becoming impatient or angry. He picked up some shells and examined them, before trying to skim them on the water. Then, he found some stones and tried again, but the sea was too unsettled for skimming and they simply splashed into the sea.

"Well, that was hopeless!" Peter said.

"It's too rough. Perhaps we should go now?"

"Soon. Look out there, there's a big swell coming in. We might have another big wave and a good receding wash. Let's wait a few minutes."

Antonia was pleased that he was trying to be supportive of her mission to see the box again. They didn't have to wait long before another huge wave started to roll in. When it crashed onto the beach, Peter got ready as the water dragged back.

"There – I can see it!" he called and dashed forward. There was the box, half in the sand. Peter pulled at it, but it wouldn't shift. The next wave was about to come in and unless he ran back up the beach, he would be soaked or even knocked over. At the last minute, he ran up to Antonia.

"Nearly. Let's wait for the next roller. I'm sure I can pull it out of the sand."

"No, Peter, it's too dangerous – there could be rip tides here. If you fell, you'd be carried away. Let's just leave it. I'm sure it's just an old coffee tin or something like that." Antonia started to wish she had never seen the box.

"One more go. Look, another swell is building," said Peter. "I think I can get it out."

The large wave came rolling in with its usual power and noise. Peter made his run before the wave started to recede: a mistake, as the force of water on the back of his legs sent him sprawling forward into the sea. He managed to scramble up, take a few steps forward and reach the box. This time, he dug his hands into the sand at the back of the box, got a good hold of the corner and pulled. The wet sand gripped the box and it took a huge effort to pull it free. The next wave hit Peter on the back and threw him towards the beach, but somehow he managed to keep his footing. He ran up the sand to where Antonia was standing.

"Bloody hell, that was an effort!" said Peter, laughing and very pleased with himself. He stood to attention and said, "Madam, may I present you with a gift from Antigua."

"Thank you, kind sir. An old tin – just what I was hoping for! But Peter, look at you, you're absolutely drenched."

"I'll soon dry out in this heat. Let's have a look at this." Peter brushed the sand off the box and held it up. "It's like a cash box – it might have once had a handle fixed here on top that has rusted off. The lid is stuck; I think it has been sealed with lead to lock it. Have a look."

Antonia took the box from Peter and immediately lifted it up to her shoulders. "It's really light – I was expecting it to be heavy." She shook the box and held it close to her ear for a clue as to what might be inside.

"The seal probably means it's airtight."

"Can't hear anything, so no gold coins, then," said Antonia.

"No, just letters, probably. Could be a deed box. It has certainly been in the sea a long time, judging by the shells stuck to it. The hurricane must have stirred up the sea so much that it exposed the box.

Look, there's an imprint of something on the lid – looks like a picture of a house, perhaps a plantation owner's mansion. We will have to clean the box up to see it clearly."

"Why don't we go over to your house? You can change into dry clothes and we can have a closer look at the box."

"Sure, let's do that."

TWELVE

Peter quickly showered and dressed in clean shorts and a T-shirt. He poured two glasses of orange juice and took them through to the living room, where Antonia sat waiting. The mysterious box was on the coffee table.

"Let me show you around the house. It won't take long, it's not a big place!" said Peter.

And he was right. Within five minutes, they were back in the living room. "We can take these out to the terrace at the back, if you like. It's in the shade."

"That would be nice," said Antonia, "and I'll bring the box."

There were two aluminium chairs and a garden table on a small tiled area. Peter grabbed two cushions for the seats from a small shed. A few plants and flowers in pots decorated the area, and a single tree at the far end added a shady, leafy canopy.

Peter brought a screwdriver from the shed and started to apply pressure to the lead seal, but with little success. He managed to scratch away a thin line of lead before saying, "I don't think I can remove the lead this way, but I might be able to force the lid open. That might damage the box a little, though, would that be OK?"

"I think so. It's already in such a poor state that we wouldn't be damaging a precious antique."

"Right, let's see." Peter found a small gap between the lid and the seal, pushed the tip of the screwdriver in and twisted it. This only bent the lip of the lid. "I'll try elsewhere." He applied more pressure to the back of the box and Peter felt the lid move. Gently working his way around the box, he could see the seal breaking away. "Here goes, I think this should do it."

With a sudden crack, the lid jumped open. Peter placed the box on the table in front of Antonia. "Have a look; let's see what these papers are all about."

Antonia carefully took out the papers. They were obviously very old, but in good condition. The seal had done its job. There was a document that looked like a deed or a certificate of ownership. The writing was faded, but perfectly legible, in the old style of a Dickensian clerk. There was a small map and a drawing of a sugar plantation windmill. The name 'Ffryes Mills' headed the drawing.

"It looks like papers detailing the title and ownership of this land shown on the map." Antonia smoothed out the papers. "It's right here on Ffryes beach – or how it looked back in the day. The deed is dated 10th August 1892. I wonder how the box came to be in the sea. Was it thrown in or did it fall from a boat? It was made to be watertight, so it seems the owner had in mind that the box might end up in the sea. What do you think?" She passed the papers to Peter.

He studied the papers quickly. "I agree. Looks like ownership papers for the land behind Ffryes beach. The boundary is shown here, look – it goes along to the far end of the beach, a long way inland on the north-east side of the road and down to the fields behind Diana's bar. And there are notes showing a plantation. Sugar, presumably. There are neighbouring plantations shown, too, going north and east along the coast and south through Darkwood. The map shows where the windmill is – just there."

"I think I've seen the windmill. When I did my nature walk with the guide, we passed a derelict windmill about a mile inland," said Antonia.

"Well, I wonder who owns the land now. There are no hotels or houses in the area, just the fields and scrubland behind."

"I could take the box to the museum in St John's and ask them to look at the papers. If they're interested, I'll donate everything to them."

"That's a good idea, Antonia. It would be interesting to know more about the history. But you know, it's curious that there is no development on this land; it would be a beautiful place to build houses or a hotel."

"Let's see what the museum people say. For now, perhaps I should be going. I'm sure you have lots to do now that the hurricane has passed," said Antonia.

Peter sat up straight. "Oh, no, not really. It would be great if you could stay for the afternoon. I've got some CDs. We could listen to music for a while before I drive you back. How does that sound?"

"Sounds great. And maybe we could walk over to the beach and watch the sunset?"

"Sure, let's do that."

After a couple of hours of relaxing, they strolled over to Ffryes. Antonia was disappointed that Peter did not take her hand and she felt a sudden worry that she had outstayed her welcome: had he really wanted her to linger after looking at the contents of the box? The sea seemed to have calmed even further, although the wind was still a steady breeze. There was a white line of clouds shading Montserrat and a few high-level wisps of cirrus out to sea. As the sun descended, the whole beach area took on a pink and gold hue.

"This is so incredible, Peter. We're lucky to have a sunset so beautiful."

"It's not like this every evening. Maybe the sunset shines on the righteous?"

They both laughed and Antonia started to walk along the water's edge towards Diana's, expecting Peter to do the same. But he turned towards Tamarind Hills and the couple bumped into each other, face to face, and giggled. Peter took Antonia in his arms and smiled at her. Antonia put her arms around Peter and felt the desire to kiss him, or be kissed.

Instead, he simply said, "It's been a wonderful afternoon, Antonia, but let's get back to the house and I will drive you home."

"Yes, of course," she said, keeping the disappointment from her voice. "I've had a great day. Thanks again for lunch. And for helping me with the mysterious box!"

"My pleasure. You must let me know what you find out about the papers."

"I will, if you would like to meet again?" Antonia said quietly.

"Of course, of course! Stupid me, I should have suggested something. Maybe next weekend, if you're free? Or during the week after work? Any time, really."

THIRTEEN

By Tuesday, almost a week after Hurricane Lorna had left Antigua, the visible effects of the hurricane had been largely cleaned up and repairs were underway to buildings in the harbour. The Ministry of Tourism team were all back in the office, busy liaising with the major hotels and tourist attractions to gauge their readiness for reopening. The airlines had started to publish flight times and the first arrivals were due the next day. The cruise ships were still at their southerly destinations, but the good news was that St John's port was undamaged and would be opening for business as soon as the new season's schedules were operational.

Antonia spent her time at work building on her tourism planning proposals for the coming season, which would start the following month in earnest with the October school holiday week. She was excited at the prospect of seeing the island in full swing: the post-pandemic global tourism industry was bouncing back and her job was to keep Antigua and Barbuda on travel agents' lists of the most attractive destinations.

She had decided not to discuss the document box with her colleagues. Something played on her mind: why had the box been sealed in the way it was? How did the current ownership of the land compare to the plans and pictures in the box? She decided to leave the matter for another day; she had something more intriguing to think about.

Peter had phoned her Monday evening, ostensibly just for a chat. They spoke about the clean-up, the good spell of weather that was forecast for the next couple of weeks, and the expected arrival of the first container ships with food, drinks and all the other supplies Antigua imported. And then Peter asked Antonia if she would like to meet for a drink after work on Wednesday. She had to hold her enthusiasm back. Instead of replying, 'I sure would!', she simply said, "Yes, thank you, that would be nice."

***

Peter parked his car in one of the spaces outside the Grouper chandlery and walked to the Mango Tree bar, where they had agreed to meet. Antonia was already seated, away from the chattering and laughter of the expat friends at the bar. She spotted him walking along the boardwalk and smiled. He wore white shorts and an expensive-looking, pale blue cotton shirt. His light suntan showed that he liked to spend time on the beach and she felt a shimmer of excitement as she gazed at his toned, supple body.

"Hi, Antonia, good to see you again. You're looking wonderful." Peter leant forward and kissed her cheek.

She was pleased he had complimented her; she had taken a long time to choose what to wear. Her dress was a simple shift in a deep coral colour, with white piping around the neck and sleeves. Its V-neck was flattering without being overly revealing and it showed off her long, shapely legs. She had her hair up in the French twist she liked.

As Peter sat down, the waiter arrived to take their drinks order – two mojitos.

"How are things at the water plant?" Antonia asked.

"Good, thanks, all back to normal now. The processing plant was undamaged in the hurricane, but some of our staff had a tough time. One lady in the admin office lost her house and has moved in with her daughter. They live in Liberta, if you know it?"

"No, I haven't been there," said Antonia.

"It's on the road to Falmouth. You might have driven through it without realising. I don't know all the history, but it was named 'Liberta' after freed slaves were able to buy their own land there in the 1800s. There are a lot of wooden houses, but also some stone-built ones. That's what my colleague's daughter has."

"It's a fascinating history. You know, I'm planning on suggesting more cultural tours to the ministry – I'm sure visitors would love to know more about the history of the places they see."

"I'm sure you're right, but is there a danger of upsetting the people who live in these towns? Some people don't like to be thought of as living specimens in a museum. I read that in some places, like South Africa and Thailand, there have been accusations of capitalising on poverty. Don't they called it township tourism – where the tour firms make money and the people are no better off?"

"Yes, I know what you mean. I've read similar things and that's definitely not what I want to promote here. It's the history of the islands that I find fascinating. Certainly is to me, anyway!"

Antonia looked at Peter. Did he seem uncomfortable? Maybe she was talking too much about work. She decided to change the subject. "Shall we look at the menu, if you're ready to eat?"

"Well, yes, if you like. I thought we were just having a couple of drinks," said Peter.

"It's no problem, if you're tight for time?"

"Oh, no, no. It would be lovely to spend the evening here."

"Do you like Caribbean food?" Antonia asked.

"I like spicy food – we could have jerk chicken with, say, rice and peas. How's that?"

"Sounds good. Perhaps a green salad as well?"

"Sure. Will you have another cocktail or a glass of wine?"

"Just a sparkling water this time, please. The cocktails are pretty punchy!"

Peter turned round to look for the waiter, who had anticipated his move and was already approaching with his notepad.

"I know what I meant to ask you," said Antonia. "Have you been to Betty's Hope?"

"No, but I've heard of it. Isn't it a restored sugar mill and museum?"

"Yes. Florence, my colleague, arranged for us to visit. It was fascinating. The museum clearly showed how tough slavery was, and even after emancipation, working conditions were really hard and dangerous. Some visitors go to the museum from the cruise ships and on tours from hotels on the island; there are very few other sites that tell the slavery story so well. I want to discuss with Aaron, my boss, how we can include more cultural activities like this in our tourism plan."

"Do you really think there will be interest? As I said, it's a sensitive subject."

"I'm not sure. Maybe I should concentrate on other initiatives."

"What do you have in mind?"

"Oh, things like music festivals, perhaps a literary week, that sort of thing. There are already sailing events and beach-focused holidays."

The waiter arrived with a tray of plates and drinks balanced on one hand. "Jerk chicken for you, guys. Good choice, here you go." He placed the dishes on the table with a flourish, poured Antonia's water and opened a bottle of Wadadli, the local beer, for Peter. Steam rose from the rice and peas, and fragrant herbs and spices that were rubbed into the chicken legs. They both commented on how sensual the flavours were – beautifully balanced, not too hot, but not at all bland. Antonia took a bite of her chicken and rice and closed her eyes in delight. The chicken was perfectly tender and the spices spread warmth in her mouth. She tasted the heat of paprika and the tang of ginger and cinnamon.

"When we've finished here, would you like a walk around the marina? There are some lovely houses and villas to see," said Antonia.

"Yes, nice idea. I've not done that before. And we can admire the yachts of the super-rich!"

In the end, their walk extended out to the residential area of the harbour. The night was dark and Peter took Antonia's arm. The breeze had dropped further. With just a quarter moon to light the sky, the stars seemed more vivid than ever, shining brightly right down to the horizon. The couple stopped and sat on a bench at the far end of the walkway, and Peter placed his arm around Antonia's waist. As she turned to face him, he leant forward and gave her a brief kiss. A thrill shot through Antonia and she closed her eyes and smiled. Peter kissed her again, more deeply, then he held her close.

Antonia was relaxed and happy. She felt that the old cliché of a couple having the right chemistry was especially true for them. She just had to be careful to manage her emotions and not fall head over heels in love with this man.

FOURTEEN

Peter had invited Antonia over for lunch the following Saturday. He had been to the Gourmand for crab meat and pasta, and had stopped off at a roadside stand to buy fresh fruit and vegetables. He planned to make crab linguini with a spicy salsa dressing, followed by papaya and mango with crème fraiche.

At half past twelve, he heard Antonia's car pull up outside and he dashed to open the door before she rang the bell. Antonia carried a small package.

After she gave Peter a brief hug, she came into the house and passed the bag to him. "Surprise! A gift from Antigua," she said.

Peter opened the bag and took out a small round box containing a rum cake. Antonia laughed. "Very thoughtful," he said. "I never would have guessed!"

"A little something special as a reward for cooking today," said Antonia. "It took me a long time to choose a gift."

Peter played along with the game – the cake was the tourists' de rigueur gift from the island and could be purchased in all the tourist shops, supermarkets and the airport. "Yes, indeed, must have taken you ages."

Antonia stepped forward and kissed him.

"Now, that's the kind of reward I like," Peter said.

They had lunch on the terrace. After they had finished, the heat of the day was at its highest, with a scorching sun and very little breeze. Peter suggested they went inside, where the air con made the temperature tolerable, and poured some cold drinks.

"Tell me, have you done anything with the box of documents we found?"

"No, not yet. I thought that I might phone the museum and book an appointment with one of their archivists."

Peter sat back. "I've been thinking about the box and why it was sealed. On a journey all the way to England, the ship's cargo could get soaked by rain or seawater in a storm. My guess is that on their way to England, something happened to the rowing boat that was carrying the papers out to the main ship. This would have been anchored somewhere offshore, a bit of a way out, and the box fell overboard without the crew noticing. Nobody raised the alarm."

"But we found the box very close to the beach. Surely if it was lost in an accident, it would have been further out?"

"Yes, that's true, but hurricanes really churn up the water and the sand. I think the box had shifted from further out to where we found it. Question is: why were the papers being sent to England, if indeed that's where they were going?"

"Yes, why should ownership papers be sent to England at all?" Antonia's curiosity was piqued.

"I'm not certain, but I think all land ownership in the colonies had to be registered in England. That could be why the box was being sent." Peter looked at his watch. "It should be a bit cooler outside now and I could do with some exercise. Why don't we go for a walk around the land shown on the map?"

"Good idea. I have a pair of trainers in my car and a sunhat."

***

As they walked past the water purification plant, Antonia said, "Just along here is where I started the nature trail walk. We went all the way up to the top of Mount Obama. Have you done the walk?"

"No, is that the one with Marley?"

"Yes – he was excellent. He knows everything about the plants and wildlife on the island."

"Yes, so I've heard, some of the people at work have mentioned him. I must do the walk with him some time. Perhaps this afternoon we can just do a couple of miles along the route. Most of the walk will be within the area shown on the old map. What do you think?"

Antonia took Peter's arm and squeezed it. "That would be lovely."

They walked along a broad dirt track that headed inland. There were some small shanty houses dotted around, with carefully tended vegetable plots. Otherwise, the land was verdant with wild bushes and grasses. Antonia pointed out a papaya tree and a bougainvillea, covered in beautiful red flowers. Less than a hundred yards off the track was a derelict sugar plantation windmill, largely covered in ivy. Parts of the walls had fallen away, but it had an improvised roof covering that must have been put there in recent times; it certainly wasn't the original.

"I wonder if that's the windmill shown on the map. Let's go and have a look inside," said Antonia, playfully pulling Peter off the track into the knee-high grass.

"Oh, I'm not sure, there might be snakes."

"Oh, come on, where's your sense of adventure? Anyway, Marley said there are no snakes on Antigua."

Peter laughed. "OK, but tread carefully."

As they approached the windmill, they could see large stones scattered around that had fallen from the mill. A doorway led into the mill. The only light came through a hole in the roof. Antonia stopped and pointed to the ground.

"Look, Peter, the grass is trodden down. Someone seems to have been here recently. There's a kind of path leading into the entrance."

"Yes, how weird. Can't think why anyone would come here."

"Young lovers, perhaps?" Antonia laughed. "I'm going to have a look inside." She picked her way through the long grass and stopped five feet from the entrance. It was so dark inside, she couldn't see a thing, so took out her phone and clicked the torch on, giving her eyes a few moments to adjust from the bright sunshine. Impatiently, she stepped forward into the doorway and felt distinctly cooler air flow past her face as it spilled out of the windmill.

"See anything?" called Peter.

"Nothing yet."

His question spurred her on and she stepped inside. A deep carpet of dried leaves crunched under her feet. A strangely sweet smell hung in the air – *perhaps the aroma of cinnamon*, she thought. Her eyes still hadn't got used to the dark, so she stood for a couple of minutes. A sudden screech split the air and Antonia froze in shock, but it was just a crow that flew up from a ridge of the windmill and disappeared through a small hole in the stonework.

Antonia gasped and her heart rate shot up, then she laughed nervously. "A bloody bird – frightened the life out of me!"

"Well, take care in there," Peter said from just outside the doorway.

Antonia waved the phone around. In the light she could see a few items of furniture that looked to have been dumped in the mill: an old rattan chair, a wooden chest, a low table. There were rotten beams of wood, a few bird feathers and a large pile of sea shells that she thought must have been washed up during a hurricane. Against the far wall was a mound of leaves, strangely well organised into a five-foot-long heap. Antonia walked over for a closer look and kicked the leaves at the edge of the heap. Her foot hit something solid and she kicked again, more firmly.

The leaves moved, uncovering something underneath. To her shock, Antonia realised it was the leg of a person.

"Peter!" she cried and jumped back. She turned and ran for the door and charged straight into Peter, who only just managed to catch her.

"Peter, there's… there's a body in there!" she screamed.

FIFTEEN

Peter gripped Antonia's shoulders and gave her a gentle shake. "Try and breathe, Antonia. Tell me exactly what you saw."

"Yes, yes." Antonia's voice was tremulous. "There's a huge pile of leaves in there. I kicked some of them around and I saw a leg – I'm sure it was. It looked like a dead body. I ran straight out; I didn't want to look any further. Peter, what are we going to do?"

"I'm going to have a look myself. If it is a body, we must call the police. Just wait here a moment."

Peter went to the doorway and, using his own phone torch, peered in. His eyes also needed time to adjust, but his impatience drove him in. He almost tripped on a length of wood, then he saw the pile of leaves. Cautiously, he stepped forward, straining to see, then swished his foot from side to side to disperse the leaves. There was nothing there. *Strange*, he thought. Perhaps Antonia had stumbled on one of the pieces of wood lying around.

"Peter, can you see anything?" Antonia called from outside.

"Not yet. I'll be out in a minute." Peter looked again at the pile of leaves, but had to conclude there was nothing to be seen. He turned to leave and as he did he got the shock of his life. In a small alcove to the left of the doorway, which he hadn't seen on his way in, sat an old woman.

"Bloody hell!" he gasped.

"Don't be frightened, man. I'm not goin' to hurt you, even though your friend woke me up," she said.

"Well, you certainly made me jump. What are you doing here?"

"I live here – well, most of the time. What brings you into my house?"

"What's going on, Peter?" The light darkened as Antonia stood in the doorway.

"There is a lady here," he called out. "She lives here. You just woke her up – she's fine."

Antonia came into the mill and saw the old woman sitting on the bench in the alcove. "Oh, thank goodness. Was it your leg I saw? I'm sorry that I kicked you," she said.

"That's no problem, girl. No damage done. But answer my question: what made you two come into the mill?"

"Curiosity," said Peter. "My friend here is interested in Antiguan history and we wanted to see what the sugar windmill looked like inside."

"Well, now you know. What's your name?" asked the old woman.

"Peter and my friend is Antonia. And your name?"

The woman straightened up, raised her eyes and said, "I'm Henrietta Foster. Most people call me Ettie. I know that some call me Mad Ettie." The woman laughed quietly to herself. "Well, Peter and Antonia, now you've seen the inside of the mill: dark and foreboding, dirty and dusty. But it's safe. I've survived many hurricanes in here!" She laughed again.

"Is this your only home? You said you lived here most of the time," Antonia said.

"You know Diana's over on Ffryes? She lets me sleep in the shed at the back of the bar sometimes. I do some cleanin' in the kitchen down there and she gives me a hot meal for my trouble. Diana nice lady, old friend."

"Yes, we know it, but don't you have a house or a family to live with?" Antonia felt concerned.

"Long time past," was all she said, then cast her eyes downwards.

Antonia felt like an intruder, bumbling into someone's home. "We'd better get going, Peter. Nice to meet you, Ettie. So sorry to have disturbed you."

They walked through the long grass back to the dirt road. "Well, that was a shock. That poor woman, living in the windmill. It hardly seems safe, but I was glad to hear she gets some support from Diana. Islanders do help each other. I wonder about her family, though."

"She was reluctant to talk about that, wasn't she? There are often outcasts in families, after a falling out or dispute. I'm not sure there's anything we can do about it."

"No, I agree," said Antonia. "Sometimes it's best not to interfere."

As they walked, Antonia named some of the plants and their uses, as Marley had explained, as medicines or foods. She wished she could remember more, especially those that were harmful if eaten or even deadly. The sky was completely clear of clouds – unusual, as there were often short, sharp showers each afternoon. The chances of a spectacular sunset were good, so Peter suggested they rest after the walk, then go over to the beach, perhaps have a drink at Diana's and watch the sun go down.

Antonia felt relaxed and happy in Peter's company. The meeting with the old lady in the windmill faded from her mind as they held hands on the water's edge and watched the sun disappear below the horizon. They then walked up the steps to the bar and found a table. Peter ordered some drinks.

Glancing around at the other guests, Antonia was delighted to see the place so busy. The tourist season was well underway and visitor numbers looked like they'd reached record levels. Bar and waiting staff hurriedly fulfilled orders, and music blared from the CD player.

"There's a great atmosphere here, Peter. We're lucky to have such a nice place local to your house."

"Yes, it's good. I guess the old woman in the mill will get some work as the season goes on."

Diana herself brought over the drinks and some complimentary dishes of nuts, olives and miniature beef patties.

Antonia smiled at her. "Can I ask you something, Diana? We met an old lady today over at the derelict windmill on a walk towards Mount Obama. She told us her name is Ettie and that she works here. What's her story? Why does she live in the mill?"

A sudden serious look crossed Diana's face. "I wouldn't worry about Ettie. She's a good person and works here part-time. We love to help her when we can, but she has some strange stories to tell and she lives in her own world."

"What do you mean?" said Antonia.

"She has some odd dreams about her family history – thinks she comes from a well-to-do background. She has no remaining family and she has been squatting in that mill for years. Every now and then the local health authorities come along and move her on, but she finds her way back again. She refuses to move into a regular house as she believes it would mean she was giving up her rights to the land."

"Rights to the land?" Antonia said quietly. "But who owns the mill and the land around it?"

"Ah, that's a good question. Ettie believes she does, but no one knows for sure. I own this little stretch of coast in between Ffryes and Coco. From time to time, property developers come along and survey the stretch of land behind Ffryes, but they never come back." Diana laughed to herself. "So our dear Ettie is safe in her windmill for a time yet!"

"Thanks, Diana." Antonia looked at Peter when Diana had gone and whispered, "I'd like to know more."

SIXTEEN

Peter was delighted that Antonia had accepted his invitation to dinner at one of the island's best restaurants. They had known each other for more than four months now and while he had very much enjoyed all the evenings out with Antonia, the beach days and their nights in cooking, he wanted to take her somewhere striking, somewhere impressive and memorable. He wanted to show Antonia how he felt about her and how important she was to him. He found it difficult to talk about his feelings and hoped the restaurant would do the talking for him. He chose a venue he had not been to before – largely because he had had no one to take to such a special place.

Antonia and Peter agreed on a Saturday evening date. Peter visited the restaurant a few days earlier to select a table with a sea view. He wanted everything to be perfect. He arranged a taxi to pick up Antonia and take her to the restaurant, a short ride from Jolly Harbour. When Antonia arrived, Peter was waiting outside to escort her through the Coco-Sand Resort, down the steep steps to the restaurant.

She's so beautiful, Peter thought.

Perched on a headland with the most magnificent views along the coast and out to sea was the aptly named Sheer Rocks. The restaurant sat at the clifftop and its tables were screened from each other with muslin curtains on a wooden framework. The curtains wafted gently in the warm breeze. The sound of waves on the shore below mixed with the chiming of a steel band from the adjacent hotel combined to make the perfect mood for a beautiful Caribbean evening. There was no moon, but the stars were so vivid that the coastline and horizon could easily be seen.

Antonia wore her favourite outfit: a close-fitting midnight-blue cotton dress, buttoned all the way down and a hem just above her knee. She wore a single row of natural pearls, a little make-up and her long brown hair was up in a ponytail. She wore shoes with a heel that made her as tall as Peter.

They sat at a small thatch-roofed bar for a drink before going to their table. Peter had a white rum and coke, but Antonia fancied a cocktail, something with a local feel. She decided on a pina colada. She was pleased with her choice, as her drink was made with a beautifully sweet, fresh pineapple.

"You look very smart tonight," said Antonia. Peter had been to St John's and treated himself to a new lime green linen shirt and white shorts. He was wearing his Breitling sports watch with a white strap and blue face, which set off his suntanned arms perfectly.

"Thanks, you look wonderful tonight. But then you always do."

"Flattery will get you everywhere."

They laughed.

"How is the tourism business coming on? There seems to be plenty of visitors around now we're in the holiday season," said Peter. "The restaurant here is full tonight – mainly with tourists, I would say."

"Things are looking great, thanks. The core attractions of the port for cruise ships and the hotel and villa operations are reporting good business, and there's the British October school holiday week of course, which is always a busy time. We're introducing more events; sailing, hosting the arrival of the trans-Atlantic rowing boats, riding, cricket and music. All happening from Christmas through to the spring. And you, how's work?" said Antonia.

"Fine, thanks. The plant is expanding its production. We're introducing more efficient technology and hoping to increase capacity by fifty per cent within two years through a new form of osmosis…" Peter stopped. "Sorry! Getting too technical there. Now that really would bore you and spoil the evening."

Antonia laughed and placed her hand on his. "It's not boring at all. I like to hear about what you do."

"But not tonight, let's enjoy the food and location." Peter picked up his menu. "What shall we have? The fish dishes look great."

"I agree, I think I'll go for the pan-fried mahi-mahi, and perhaps we can share some olives and bread to start," said Antonia. "How about you?"

"I like the sound of the lobster tail ravioli with a green salad. And shall I order a bottle of wine? White?"

"Yes, perfect."

The waitress took their order and they sat back and looked out to sea. A few small lights showed that there were boats on the move, while a long way out they could see the bright block of lights that was a cruise ship on its inter-island journey.

"This is a beautiful place, Peter. Thank you so much for suggesting we come here."

After their meal, Peter took Antonia's hands in his and leant across the table. "Meeting you, Antonia, and getting to know you has been so unexpected. I was becoming resigned to never finding anyone I wanted to spend time with. I hope I'm not overthinking this, but I do want to see you more. I hope you feel the same."

"Oh, Peter, of course I do, but we've only known each other a few months, so let's take our time and see where it goes, get to know each other better. We've both been in relationships before that didn't work out. Neither of us wants to be hurt."

"You're right, it's best to take our time. Having said that, I wanted to ask if you'd like to go to Shirley Heights tomorrow evening for the music and something to eat. But I understand if you think two dates in a weekend would be too much of a good thing!"

Antonia laughed gently. "No, that would be great. I've heard about the Sunday evening parties down there and it would be nice to go. I wonder if the food will be as good as tonight. It has been wonderful."

"Maybe not – an open-air barbecue might not be up to tonight's standards!"

After their main courses, they both chose a passionfruit mousse and a glass of Sauternes. As the waitress left with their order, they held hands again. Peter's eyes met Antonia's. Nothing needed to be said; they smiled lovingly at each other.

***

Peter suggested they walk back to his house for coffee and a nightcap. He would call a taxi to take Antonia home from there. Although it was still perfectly warm, Antonia took out the thin cotton scarf she had placed in her handbag. Peter unfolded the colourful square and wrapped it around Antonia's shoulders. She looked across at him and smiled. The sound of the sea faded as they walked inland. Antonia found the rustling of the trees in the wind and the chirping of the countless little tree frogs mesmerising.

"There's so much wildlife here," she said. "It sounds like each of the frogs has a tiny bell he is ringing. And the parrots are having a lovely conversation!"

"Yes, the jungle comes alive at night. Humans sleep, wildlife runs around. Funny, isn't it?"

Antonia didn't answer; she just smiled at Peter and touched his hand. As they arrived at the house, Peter unlocked the door and switched on the lights. "Go through. I'll put the coffee on. And I have a lovely Zacapa rum if you'd like a glass to go with your coffee?"

"That would be nice, thanks. Just a small one."

"There are some CDs next to the TV, if you would like to put something on?"

"I'll have a look." Antonia found a compilation album of Cuban music, salsa and samba. The tunes were slow and melodic, perfect for late at night. Peter brought in the coffee and rum.

Antonia sipped her rum. "Wow, that's gorgeous, so smooth."

They drank the coffee and Peter refilled their glasses with another small shot of rum and ice.

"Do you dance, Peter?"

"Badly, I'm afraid. I used to go to a salsa club when I was at university. What about you?"

In response, Antonia stood up and held out her hand. "Well, let's give it a go!" she said, laughing as she pulled Peter up.

They danced a slow salsa. Peter held Antonia close and she rested her head on his shoulder. The warmth of the night, the meal, the rum… they had all made Antonia relaxed and happy. Peter gave Antonia a long, lingering kiss, then trailed kisses along her shoulder and neck as he stroked her back. As they danced, her eyelashes fluttered against his cheek. He lifted her hand and softly bit her fingers, then led her to the bedroom.

SEVENTEEN

"Antonia, would you like to take a break? Go for coffee, perhaps?"

The Ministry of Tourism office was quietly humming with staff concentrating on their work. Most were on computers, a couple were on the phone and Aaron was in his office with two government officials discussing tourist numbers.

"Sure, that would be great, Florence. Shall we go down into the marina?" Antonia grabbed her notebook and pen and placed them in her shoulder bag.

After a short walk, they found a table at the far end of the boardwalk in the shade.

"It's good to see the marina so busy," said Florence.

"Yes, the season's going well. Feedback from the hotel association is excellent, with some reporting record room occupancy."

"Indeed and the next big busy time will be Christmas. Do you have any plans to take time off?" Florence asked.

"I haven't really thought about it. I told my mother before I left that I wouldn't be coming home for Christmas…" Antonia stopped short, wondering where home really was. "Back to the UK, I mean," she said, quietly. "But I have a brother, younger than me, and he and his family will be with my parents on Christmas Day, so I'll give them a call on Christmas morning."

"Not many staff take time off during the busy period, so that's great. I will make up a schedule so that we can be sure the office is staffed at all times."

"Good plan," said Antonia.

"And there's something else. Aaron has asked me to arrange a team outing for next week. We're going to charter *Happy Days* – you might have seen the boat in the marina? It's a beautiful luxury motor yacht."

"Yes, I have – very nice. Which day are you planning?"

"A week on Friday. We will meet around ten thirty, motor around the island, stop for swimming and beach fun, then have lunch somewhere nice. And we can bring a partner or friend, anyone you like."

"Sounds brilliant."

"Do you have someone you would like to bring? You don't have to of course, several of the staff will be on their own. I have to ask so that we get the numbers right." Florence spoke slowly, the trace of a smile on her lips. "But am I right in thinking there is someone special in your life at the moment?"

Antonia was stunned; she hadn't spoken about Peter to anyone in the office. "Well, maybe there is – hey, come on, Florence, how did you know?"

"Like I've said before, it's island life. Nothing stays a secret!" Florence patted Antonia's hand and smiled. "Some of my friends saw you at Sheer Rocks, they work there."

"Ha! Of course, island life. I'm not hiding anything; I just haven't felt the time was right to mention Peter to you."

"I didn't mean to be intrusive…"

"Oh, no, it's alright. In fact, it would be great if Peter could come on the boat trip. I will ask if he can make it. Can you give me a day or two?"

"Sure, I will reserve two places for you. Now, come on, girl, tell me about Peter! Where did you meet him? What's he like?"

Antonia told Florence how she had met Peter on Ffryes beach and again at the Gourmand. She mentioned the bars and restaurants they had been to, as well as where Peter worked. She felt that her chat with Florence helped to deepen their friendship; she didn't really have any close female friends on the island. And she was very happy to talk about Peter: it made her think about how she felt and where their relationship was going.

***

That evening, Antonia called Peter at home. After catching up on their working days, Antonia mentioned the trip on the boat. At first, Antonia couldn't help thinking Peter sounded cautious – perhaps he didn't feel ready to be seen as her partner. This would be the first function they would attend as a couple – was he uncomfortable with that? Peter asked several questions about the plans for the day and who might be on the trip, before the tone of his voice changed and he enthusiastically said that he'd love to come and he was looking forward to it.

Peter also asked Antonia if she would like to spend Saturday afternoon at Darkwood beach, just a mile further on from Ffryes where the sea was likely to be calm and the water crystal clear. They could take a picnic lunch and walk to the far end of the beach where there was an excellent spot for snorkelling among the rocks. They would see shoals of beautiful tropical fish and maybe a turtle or two. Antonia accepted immediately and said she would call into the Grouper chandlery and buy a full face mask with a fitted snorkel. Peter also recommended that she buy a UV protection swim shirt – he knew how powerful the sun would be on her back.

Antonia was delighted that Peter would be joining her on the yacht. It made their relationship feel more official somehow. She hoped Peter was happy with that – he had sounded unsure, reluctant to accept the invitation. She told Florence that Peter would be coming along and asked what she should wear. Florence didn't hesitate: beach wear and a wrap on the boat to keep the sun off, then shorts and a smart top for the restaurant.

"I'll see what I have in my wardrobe," said Antonia.

"We have a meeting planned at the port offices in St John's on Friday," said Florence with a conspiratorial smile. "I'm sure there will be time for some clothes shopping then. Shall we do that?"

"Brilliant idea!" Antonia was delighted with the suggestion. She was pleased that her friendship with Florence was developing. Her relationship with Peter was wonderful, but it was nice to have a woman's company at times.

EIGHTEEN

Peter was surprised. Soon after he'd arrived at work, George Robartes, the chief scientist, asked him to join him for coffee in his office. Assuming it was for a discussion on the water output for the previous week, Peter picked up the file with the figures, his notebook and a newly sharpened pencil.

After pouring them coffee, George sat down, made a pyramid with his fingers and pursed his lips, but said nothing for a few moments. Then, he cleared his throat. "I have some news, Peter. As you know, I will be coming up for retirement in a year's time, but there has been a change of plan. The directors want to start recruiting my successor now. They have asked me to draw up a list of candidates. Naturally, you will be on the list, given your career to date and the excellent work you have been doing in Antigua."

"Thanks, George, good of you to say so. This comes as quite a surprise. I thought that a new chief scientist would be appointed about this time next year."

"So did I, but the directors want to submit a bid for World Bank Caribbean funding to extend the plant and they believe it's vital to have the new chief in place before they submit the bid. The money will help us develop the plant and keep up with demand for water. Hence the need to move things along more quickly."

"I see. Makes sense." said Peter. He was not happy with this news, but was relieved that he would be considered for the role, given the relatively short time he had been working at the plant.

"To get the recruitment process going, I will be drafting a job description and person specification and I'll send these to a firm of headhunters based in Miami. The board members feel that access to candidates from the US will be important. Now, am I right in assuming that you would like to apply, Peter? I have to ask."

"Of course; it's what I have been working towards. I feel it's a natural career move, one that I'm ready for – and what better place is there to live and work? Although you and I have never talked about it directly, one of the key things that brought me to Antigua was the prospect of being appointed chief scientist after your retirement. I guess I have been foolish to assume that the job would automatically be mine."

"Well, off the record, I believe you have all the attributes required for the job. My advice would be to apply with all the commitment you showed when you applied for your current job. You have every chance of success, but the directors need to demonstrate they have been thorough in appointing my successor – you know how banks like to see due process."

"I do indeed."

"Right then. I'll get on with the job and person spec and let you know how matters progress. Expect to be contacted by the headhunters, as they will be carrying out the initial interviews for all candidates. And feel free to discuss the process with me at any time."

"Will do, thanks George."

Peter went back to his desk in a state of shock. He'd expected more time to build his reputation as the natural successor to Robartes. He still felt confident that his experience and technical knowledge would put him up there as the best candidate for the job, but now the odds would be stacked against him, with more contenders to be considered. He thought about what his future would hold if he didn't get the job; he would be stuck in the number two position in the organisation, having to work for someone he might, or might not, get on with.

A sudden sinking feeling came over him: he realised that if he wasn't selected he might not have a future on the island – and what did that mean for his relationship with Antonia? She was committed to living on the island and if he didn't have the job he wanted, it could mean him looking elsewhere; Australia again, or the Middle East, perhaps. There were plenty of opportunities in many of the Arab countries and Israel, of course. Or perhaps he would even return to the UK. He resolved to hold back, not to let his feelings run away with him, not to fall hopelessly in love with Antonia. And he didn't want to carry on letting her believe they had a long-term future in Antigua. Peter knew he had to be honest with her and tell her about the change to his prospects of staying on the island. The question was: when?

NINETEEN

Peter found a parking space just behind Antonia's apartment block and ran up the stairs to her door. He was ten minutes late. He looked carefully at Antonia to see if she was irritated by his lateness, and was pleased and relieved that she seemed unconcerned. Apologising profusely, and taking Antonia's canvas beach bag, he led the way back down the stairs and out onto the harbour. A group of Antonia's colleagues were just boarding *Happy Days*. Florence held her phone to her ear. As they arrived, Florence said, "Ah, there you are! I was just trying to call you."

"Sorry, we were running a bit late," said Antonia. "Florence, this is Peter."

"Very pleased to meet you, Peter." Florence held out her hand and gave Peter her best smile and a flutter of her eyes. "Have a great day! I'll introduce you to Aaron and the others once we get underway."

The captain, smartly dressed in a white officer's shirt and tailored navy shorts, called out to a crewman, who untied the ropes. Antonia was spellbound for a moment as she recognised the crewman – he was one of the 'international couple' she had seen sitting at the bar at Diana's.

With a quiet purr of the engines, the motor yacht pulled away from the jetty and turned towards the harbour entrance. The crewman joined the captain on the bridge and unfolded a chart of the local waters. A few minutes later, they passed the last of the villas surrounding the marina and headed towards the open sea. The captain took a microphone off the dashboard and spoke to the guests.

"Good morning, everyone. I'm Captain Thomas and I would like to welcome you onto *Happy Days* and introduce you to our second-in-command, Mike, who will be helping us today. Also Tamsin, our lovely head of guest services. Sit back, relax and enjoy your day – we will do our best to make it truly one of your happy days!"

As they cruised along, Tamsin brought round a tray of drinks: orange and mango juice, beer and, of course, flutes of champagne. Once everyone was served, Florence asked Antonia and Peter to join her in the seats beside the bridge to meet Aaron.

The two men shook hands. "Great to meet you, Peter. I'm Aaron Jaygo. I gather you live on the island."

"Yes, I've been here more than a year now. I work at the Dart Water Health plant near Ffryes."

"I know it – my good friend, George Robartes, runs the place. In fact, we are old friends. We went to school together, but he was the brainy one and went off to England to study. We meet at the cricket ground from time to time and at a card school in St John's. A very nice chap."

"He certainly is. He's my immediate boss."

"Really? You must be very high up in the ranks, Peter! With high ambitions?"

"Well, perhaps," Peter said, not entirely sure why he felt uncomfortable with the discussion. Was his suitability for Antonia being judged? Or was his fitness for a senior role at the water company being assessed?

"And isn't George retiring soon?" said Aaron.

Peter froze. He hadn't discussed his news about the retirement with Antonia nor what it might mean for him if he didn't get the top job. "Yes, next year some time, I gather," he said, deliberately being vague. 'Next year' could be a few months or more than twelve months away. "You must be the same age – are you thinking of retiring?"

"Oh no, there's too much to do developing tourism on the island. It's a very competitive business in the Caribbean," Aaron said reflectively. "There are new opportunities developing every year here on Antigua and Barbuda."

"We are seeing that at the water plant – huge demands for fresh water. It's a struggle to keep up." Peter glanced at Antonia and was relieved to see that she looked calm, unworried. He told himself he would have to tell her as soon as possible that his future on the island was uncertain.

"Have a great trip, both of you. I just need to check today's itinerary with the captain. I'll join you when we reach our first stop." Aaron turned and stepped up onto the bridge.

Antonia was very glad Aaron was being so friendly. She didn't really see him as an outgoing person; he was somewhat quiet and reserved. It was important for her job that she got on well with him and so far he had been polite, but not overly supportive of some of her ideas. Antonia felt that Aaron might struggle with change. She and Peter walked to the back of the boat, found a couple of seats and quickly fell into lively discussion about the day ahead with the other guests.

The boat headed north, passing the harbour of St John's. After only an hour, they turned into a small bay and Mike, the crewman, dropped the anchor. Florence called out for everyone's attention. "I hope you enjoyed our little cruise," she said. "Now it's time for a swim and snorkelling – or you can stay on the boat if you're not feeling energetic!"

Most people were wearing their swimming kit under their clothes. They undressed, then stepped down to the rear platform and slipped into the sea.

Antonia and Peter had brought their own snorkelling masks. They swam away from the boat across the bay. The water was crystal clear. Small shoals of fish darted around the rocks strewn across the bottom of the sea, just ten feet below them. Antonia suddenly caught hold of Peter's arm and pointed. Towards the headland at the end of the beach, they saw the languid movements of a turtle, swimming low down and grazing on plants growing on the rocks. The couple swam slowly towards it. A shaft of sunlight penetrated the water, brightening its mottled green and brown back. They got too close and the turtle simply waved its flippers and moved away. Then, they found a group of blue angelfish; nervous of the snorkellers, they dashed away in a synchronised shoal.

After the swim, the guests all had a quick shower onboard and dressed for lunch. The tender took them ashore in threes and fours, and soon everyone was standing in the bar at the Casa Blanca restaurant. A long table had been laid so all the guests could sit together. Antonia and Peter sat at one end of the table, opposite Florence. Aaron presided over the lunch with a seat in the centre. The starters came promptly: seafood platters to share and home-baked bread. A choice of lamb curry or prawn salad followed by lime crème brûlée and fruit salad. Coffee and chocolates rounded off the meal.

Having enjoyed a great lunch and plenty of drinks, no one was enthusiastic about taking part in the beach sports that Florence had suggested. Instead, the restaurant had a small dance floor and a few of the members of staff went over to dance to the music that had been turned a little louder. Antonia noticed Florence looking at Peter with a faint smile. When a lively samba started to play, she went over and asked him to dance. Antonia knew he wasn't the world's best dancer, but he keenly accepted her offer. The couple stayed on the floor for a second track, then Florence gave Peter a kiss on the cheek and led him back to the table. Antonia felt a pang of disappointment that Peter didn't ask her to dance, but thought that he had accepted a dance or two with Florence to be sociable at Antonia's work event.

The afternoon drifted on, with the group enjoying a few more drinks and relaxed conversation on the terrace. Around 4 p.m. Mike came to the restaurant entrance and caught Florence's eye – it was time to board the boat and return to Jolly Harbour.

Peter found himself a seat at the rear, allowing Antonia the space to enjoy the company of her work colleagues – after all, the trip was a team-building exercise. He was surprised when Aaron came to join him. Peter found it difficult to make conversation with Aaron, soon discovering they had little in common, and so he stuck to predictable questions. Where do you live? How long have you been with the ministry? Have you been on this boat before? Aaron said his family used to live at Liberta, but he now had a house near Falmouth, overlooking the harbour. Peter knew enough of the area to realise that was a very expensive location. He wondered momentarily where Aaron had got the money to buy a property there. Liberta was one of the original settlements for freed slaves and not one of the most attractive places nowadays. Aaron had made quite a step up.

But Aaron seemed a little worse for wear after all the drinks at lunch. He sat back and pointed at Peter. "You and Antonia are doing good work here in Antigua, but we don't want to be reminded that we were once slaves to the British and they owned the island. We are blessed with a beautiful place to live and tourism is vital to our economy. Real money can only be made by focusing on the luxury end of the market and these people don't want to spend time going around the poorer villages on the island and learning about the slavery history. And believe me, people in the villages don't want to have foreigners eyeballing them."

Peter realised that Aaron was telling him something he might not have told Antonia. Why was this? Why was he seemingly reluctant to discuss this with her?

"There are plans for some classy new hotels and resorts," Aaron continued, "but Antigua has strong competition in the Caribbean. It needs to become known as the destination for the discerning traveller. It will all lead to worthwhile employment – for everyone on the island."

Peter felt he should do more than mumble agreement and smile politely; silence would be a betrayal to Antonia. "But isn't it a changing world for the tourism industry? It seems to me that the two can prosper together: high-end locations with cultural dimensions that those discerning travellers can enjoy. They are, after all, thinking people, with wide interests and the money to spend on informative guided tours."

"No, no, it doesn't work like that. My vision of the luxury end of the market is for hotels, spas, resorts that people won't want to leave."

Peter concluded that pursuing the discussion would be counter-productive. "Right, I see," was his diplomatic response.

As the boat headed south-west, the sun shone directly onto them and Aaron pulled his hat low over his face. He let his eyes close and the conversation came to an end. Peter was relieved. It was becoming tense and he didn't want to say anything that would antagonise Antonia's boss – she had enough on her plate working with this man.

As he admired the scenery, the sun was suddenly blocked. He looked up and saw Florence, holding two tall glasses. She handed one to him. "Here, enjoy a Caribbean special – papaya, mango and pineapple with a touch of spiced rum."

Peter stood up and took a sip. "Thanks, that's delicious. Tastes like more than a touch of rum, though."

Florence laughed. "Well, you have to get the right vibes on a boat like this."

"Yes, true. It's been a great day. Thanks for inviting me."

"No problem. It has been a pleasure to meet you." Florence brushed her hand along Peter's arm, just as Antonia arrived beside them.

"Having a good time, Peter?" she asked. Peter wondered if there was a touch of sarcasm in her voice. "What's that you're drinking?"

Florence smiled. "It's a spiced rum punch. Can I get you one?"

"Thanks, that would be great."

As Florence went to the bar, Antonia put her arm around Peter's waist and squeezed him close to her.

"It's been a great day. Have you enjoyed yourself, darling?" said Antonia.

"Yes, really good but I'm looking forward to getting you to myself…"

TWENTY

Antonia invited Peter back to her flat after the cruise and put on the coffee machine. She was tired, but happy that the day had gone so well. Peter came out to the kitchen and hugged her.

"While you're here, there's something I'd like to show you," she said. "I've had another look at the papers we found at Ffryes beach." Antonia took some rolled sheets of vellum from the tin, yellow with age but perfectly preserved and readable, and smoothed them out flat on the dining table. "This seems to be the ownership deed for the area of land shown on the map and here's a receipt for the sale of the land. There's a letter to a firm of solicitors in Wells in Somerset called Carter, Kingsnorth that asks for the sale to be registered."

"That's interesting. May I see?" Peter picked up the document and read aloud the opening sentences. "… and let it be recorded that the first party, namely Arthur Arkwright, resident of Crab Ridge Estate, Antigua, and of the town of Wells, in the county of Somerset, England, in consideration of the payment of one pound, duly received this day of signature, has willingly entered an agreement for the sale and transfer of the freehold of the estate known as Ffryes Mills, and it is noted that the ownership of the estate shall vest in the second party, namely Nathaniel Foster, citizen of Antigua, on the twenty-first day of October in the year of our Lord 1892. Such freehold to be held in perpetuity." Peter paused. "The deed is dated the fourteenth of October."

"Why only one pound?" said Antonia.

"Any amount paid validates the contract. If nothing is paid at all, then the contract of sale is void. Sometimes you see the payment of a peppercorn, meaning a small amount that nevertheless has value. In effect, the land was given away, but the contract for sale is valid."

"Right. But if these papers didn't make it to England, then the ownership of the estate might never have been registered," said Antonia. "Question is: who owns the land now? The people at the museum in St John's might know – I still haven't been in touch with them. If these documents should have been sent to England, there might be a copy held somewhere. I wonder if they're open tomorrow, it's Saturday. Let's look up their website. Yes, here we are… open 10 a.m. until 1 p.m."

"Ah, I have a team meeting in the morning at the plant. I won't be able to come with you," Peter said.

"Well, let's go some other time," said Antonia. "But what I would like to do tomorrow afternoon, if you're free, is go to Darkwood beach again. The weather has been so good that the water will be calm and clear – great for swimming and snorkelling. Would that be OK?"

"Perfect. I should be finished at the plant by midday – perhaps we can have lunch at the little bar at the back of the beach?"

"Oh, we can get some drinks from the bar, but I'd like to bring lunch."

"Even better idea! I shall look forward to it." Peter smiled.

***

After Peter had left, Antonia looked at the papers again. She studied the map carefully and compared the boundary of the estate with the modern-day use of the land. There were no buildings present other than the dilapidated windmill and the land was not farmed. It was in effect deserted or abandoned. Her curiosity was piqued. The Tamarind Hills development was a significant investment in luxury real estate at the southern end of Ffryes and Diana said that she owned the land at the northern headland, where her restaurant was. Beyond the boundary of the map on the land side sat Peter's water processing plant. And that was it. No other development had ever been undertaken on Ffryes Mills.

Antonia wondered if Florence might know the history of the area. She wanted to talk to her about it, but she felt hesitant as she would have to mention the discovery of the box. For reasons she couldn't quite put her finger on, she didn't want to do this.

She collected the papers from the table to replace in the box. She decided to read the letter to the solicitors in Wells again. She ran her eyes quickly over the beautiful handwriting, and suddenly she stopped, shocked, realising what she was reading. "The ownership of the estate vested in one Nathaniel Foster," she said. "But that's Ettie's surname. She's Henrietta Foster!"

TWENTY-ONE

Peter slept badly after the day out on the yacht, plagued by the anxiety he felt about applying for George's job and his prospects on Antigua if he failed to get the promotion. After Aaron's comments about George Robartes' retirement, Peter realised it was now public knowledge that his replacement would have to be found.

They had only been together for four months, but he was deeply in love with Antonia, and if she felt the same, then surely they would find a way to be together. But if he didn't get the job, their future would be uncertain. He knew that Antonia saw her life and career as being in Antigua. Would she throw it all away for the sake of their relationship? Or would he decide it was better for him to keep his current job as second-in-command and be happy with Antonia? He resolved to talk to her before they went to Darkwood beach.

After the meeting at the plant, during which Peter could hardly think straight, he was relieved to get out of the office and back to his house. Just minutes after he arrived, Antonia pulled up in her car and came to the door, carrying a wicker picnic basket.

Peter opened the door and smiled at her. He thought she looked wonderful: her hair was up in a French twist and her sarong, a deep sea-green, matched the colour of her eyes.

"How was your morning?" asked Antonia.

"Oh… not bad. And you, have you been busy?"

"Not really, to be honest. But Peter, I've been reading the papers from the box again and I've noticed something really exciting!" Antonia had a broad smile on her face. Before Peter could say anything, she went on, "Remember the letter to the solicitors in Wells, about the sale of the land?"

"Yes, to er, Nathaniel Foster, wasn't it?"

"Yes, and you remember the old woman we found in the windmill? Well, her name is Ettie Foster. That's got to be more than a coincidence, hasn't it? And Diana mentioned that Ettie says she comes from a wealthy family. I think we should go and see her again and ask her what her story is, find out whether she knows anything about the history of Ffryes Mills. Maybe she really is the rightful owner of the land!"

Peter laughed. "It certainly is a fascinating thought that she would be the current owner. But really, is that likely? It would be a hell of a coincidence."

Antonia picked up in his tone an apparent indifference about the papers. "Agreed, but aren't you keen to know more?" she said.

"Sorry, yes. Yes I am, but can we talk about this later? I have some work news that I need to discuss with you."

"Why don't we get down to the beach before it gets too busy, find a good spot under a sunshade and talk about it then? And we can have a chat about Ettie – it's incredible to think that she could be related to Nathaniel Foster!" Antonia laughed and leant forward to kiss Peter on the cheek.

He could see the time wasn't right for him to break the news about his job. He already had his beach gear in a bag by the door. "OK, sure, let's get over there. Here, let me put the basket in the car."

They found a great spot at the far end of the beach and grabbed one of the few unoccupied sunshades. From here, they could walk directly into the sea to swim and snorkel. Antonia suggested they start with a leisurely swim to build up their appetite for lunch. They swam out to the rocks at the corner of the bay. Peter held onto an outcrop that protruded just above the surface and turned to look for Antonia. Right behind him, she followed suit. She swept her wet hair back from her face and smiled at Peter. He felt a rush of love for Antonia; she was so beautiful and she loved to do the things he enjoyed. They were so suited together as a couple. They both had good jobs and Antigua, with its warm sea, white sand and sunshine, was the right environment for them to live a good life. While they rested and caught their breath, he realised that he could see them spending their lives together. He leant over to her and kissed her, then pulled her gently towards the shore. She took the hint and they swam back to the beach. While Peter went to buy drinks at the bar, Antonia spread out the picnic blanket and took out the food.

"What a great way to spend a Saturday afternoon," said Peter.

"Yes, it's wonderful here."

After the meal, Peter stretched out and closed his eyes, almost drifting off to sleep. Antonia lay next to him and wrapped her arms around him. He could hear the satisfying sound of the sea gently lapping and the palm trees rustling in the breeze. A distant child's laughter carried along the beach. He heard Antonia whisper, "I love you, my darling."

"And I love you," he said.

Antonia laughed. "You weren't supposed to hear that! I thought you were asleep. I'm sorry, I don't want to complicate things between us, but that's how I feel."

Peter opened his eyes. "Oh, Antonia, I'm so glad you feel like that. And so I'll say it again – I love you."

Antonia smiled and kissed him. Peter had never felt so happy. However, in the same way that the afternoon rain clouds were now blocking out the sun, his happiness was shadowed by the need to discuss his job prospects with Antonia – but not right now. It could wait.

***

Back at his house that evening, over a glass of chilled white wine, Peter remembered that Antonia had wanted to talk about the papers in the box and how they might be connected with Ettie. She said that she wanted to go and see her again at some point the following weekend to get Ettie's story first-hand. In the meantime she would call into the museum and try to find out more about how property was owned and sold back in the 1890s.

Peter knew that Antonia was inquisitive and curious. She would not let the mystery of Ettie and the Ffryes Mills estate rest. It was as if she was a detective on an investigation, seeking out evidence, the truth, justice. He wondered where she got her determination and strength of character from. He was captivated and decided he would do all he could to support her in the case.

TWENTY-TWO

"How was your weekend, Florence?" Antonia asked as they sat down in their usual seats in the shade. They had gone to the Mango Tree for morning coffee.

"Good, thanks. It was my mother's birthday last week so we had family over for lunch yesterday. Great to see some of my aunts and cousins again. What about you? What did you do? Did you meet up with Peter?"

"Yes, on Saturday. He was working in the morning, so we went to Darkwood for the afternoon. Great swimming and snorkelling among the rocks."

"Is Peter a good swimmer? I guess he should be. He looks very fit," said Florence with a smile.

"Yes… yes, he is. And it's a really good spot to see fish."

"Did you see any turtles?"

"No, but lots of lovely rainbow-coloured fish, only three or four inches long, swimming in huge shoals. And a few pretty angelfish, mainly blue and gold, some green, nibbling at the rocks."

"Sounds great. You should buy an underwater camera!"

"Yes, good idea. Then in the evening we looked through some old papers we found at Ffryes a few weeks ago."

"Really? What are they and how did you find them?"

Antonia hesitated, realising she had not told Florence about the papers. But now she had mentioned it, she felt she had to continue. "Ah yes, I haven't told you about this. Just after the hurricane, Peter and I were walking along Ffryes beach when we saw an old tin box stuck in the sand. When the waves went out, Peter was able to go and grab it. We took it back to his house and opened it. That was tough, because the box was very old and sealed shut. But inside, perfectly preserved, was a collection of old papers relating to the ownership of land near Ffryes beach. All dated back to the 1890s. There was a deed, a map and a letter to a solicitor in Wells, a town in England."

"How amazing! What were the papers about?"

Antonia suddenly realised it would be a mistake to connect the papers with who she and Peter had found in the windmill. It might not be a good thing for Ettie if people started to take an interest in her. And she wanted to visit the museum first to try to verify the information.

"Not much, really. Just some drawings of the area, some papers I can hardly read. I'm planning on taking them along to the national museum in St John's, either for some advice or to leave the box and the documents with them. In fact, I hope they will help me with my research into the slavery and emancipation idea that I've been working on." Antonia felt pleased with the subtle change of subject.

"Ah, yes. I'm glad you brought that up." Florence's face changed from her usual positive, smiling demeanour to a worried frown. "Not everyone is happy with the concept."

"You mean Aaron?" said Antonia.

"Yes, exactly. Knowing Aaron, I feel he has been humouring you since you raised the subject, hoping you'd forget about the idea. He has ambitions for Antigua to be known as the highest of high-end destinations, which is great of course, but social and historical tourism? Forget it. That's not on his agenda. You might find it hard to get his support for your ideas."

"Thanks for the heads-up, Florence. I don't want to antagonise the boss – and although I'm hugely interested in history, and Antiguan history in particular, I'm not so keen on cultural tourism that I'm going to risk falling out with Aaron over it. It's not worth it. I guess I'll treat my interest in history as a hobby, something to do off duty."

"Makes sense. You will have the best of both worlds: a happy boss and an interest to follow!" Florence's smile had returned.

Antonia looked at her watch. "We had better get back. But thanks, Florence. It's great to have your advice. You're a good friend."

However, as they walked back, Antonia felt a hollowness in the pit of her stomach. Could she really trust Florence? She was a beautiful woman who had shown too much interest in Peter...

TWENTY-THREE

As the tourism season progressed, which coincided with a prolonged dry spell, the need for fresh water on the island steadily increased. The output from the reverse osmosis plant was near its maximum and would struggle to cope with any more demand; the situation clearly showed that the expansion of the plant was a priority in the long term. The board of directors wanted to see contingency plans for restricting the supply of water to the population, should this become necessary. George Robartes assigned the task to Peter.

This was the type of work he enjoyed: building a coherent management plan based on a scientific analysis of the flow-through of source water and delivery to the supply system. Not an easy task, as the plans could well include shutting down the water supply for short periods, upsetting the local community and businesses. But Peter had devised a plan that factored in the plant doing extra processing during the late evening and into the night. It just needed a skeleton staff to oversee the machinery and bonuses would be paid to staff who volunteered for these shifts. There was no shortage of employees who would come forward. Peter's detailed financial analysis showed that the extra staff costs would be less than the plant would lose from temporary shutdowns. The board supported his package of proposals.

George Robartes caught Peter just as he was about to go to lunch. "That was a great submission to the board, Peter. The directors were very pleased with your recommendations and have given the go-ahead. This will stand you in good stead for your application for my role after I retire."

"Thanks, George. I applied, as you know, but I've heard nothing from the headhunters. Any idea of how the process is going?"

"Yes, a shortlist has been provided to the chairman. In confidence, I can confirm that your name is on the list. There are six candidates. The interview dates are being sorted out right now and you should hear soon. But remember, although I'm on the selection panel, the final decision will be the chairman's. There are some American nationals on the list and one Antiguan, who currently lives and works in California. He must have a good chance. For any overseas candidate, it's important that the board is confident they will be able to relocate to the island."

"As I have done," said Peter.

"Indeed! You have settled in very well, so much so I would call you an honorary Antiguan." George smiled. "Look, be confident. You have a lot to offer Dart Water and I believe the directors know that. They will have to run their preferred candidate past the World Bank people – it wouldn't do to appoint a chief scientist who didn't meet their expectations."

"Makes you wonder who's running this business, the board or the all-powerful money men."

"Well, that's a fair point, but you understand that financial management is just as much a part of running the business as good science."

"Yes, that's true. Thanks for the update, George. I'll give it my best shot when we get to the interviews."

***

Back at his desk, Peter suddenly felt depressed. His job prospects were uncertain, which meant his life on the island was uncertain, and the most significant and potentially painful outcome was the end of his relationship with Antonia. He knew that he had taken any excuse not to talk to Antonia about his job interview and the time had come to face up to the consequences, whatever they were. Being in love and in a partnership meant being open and honest, and he was failing on both counts. He found his phone and sent her a text.

Hi darling, are you free this evening? Need a chat xx

Yes, sure. Problem?

Not really. Just need to tell you about what's going on here at work. Could affect my job. Straight from work OK?

OK, I'll meet you at the Mango Tree.
I'll try and get there for 5.30. Love you xx

Peter passed the afternoon in a daze. Trying to concentrate on spreadsheets of water flows, electricity costs, supply peaks and future demand trends was next to impossible, and he was glad when the clock ticked round to 5 p.m. He mentioned to the works manager that he had to leave early and walked quickly back to his house to get his car. He arrived at Jolly Harbour with five minutes to spare, found a table and waited for Antonia to arrive, nervous as hell. He breathed deeply as his heart beat at twice its normal rate. He didn't have long to wait, as he soon saw Antonia coming along the boardwalk.

"Hi, Peter, lovely to see you." Antonia leant across the table and they kissed.

"And you. What would you like to drink?"

"A fruit punch would be nice, thanks."

"Me too, I think."

The ever-attentive waiter arrived and took the order.

"So, what's happening at work? Is the price of water going up?" Antonia laughed. Peter thought she looked nervous – she was probably curious about what he was going to say.

"That would be good. No, something more serious, at least for me. You know I have been here for over a year and one of the reasons I took the job was that George Robartes, my boss, the chief scientist, is due to retire next year? By then, I will have been working for two years as his deputy and I was hoping to get his job when he retired. No, it's more than that: I was expecting to be given the job. Problem is, George's retirement date has been brought forward to early next year, about three or four months from now, and the directors have started to recruit a new chief scientist. It's all to do with World Bank Caribbean funding for the expansion of the plant."

Antonia's smile faded. She placed her hands on Peter's. "But surely that's only a formality? You will be promoted, won't you?"

"I'm not sure. An outside firm of headhunters has been appointed and they're recruiting candidates from the US. Apparently, they have a shortlist drawn up already."

"And your name is on it?"

"Yes, but the chance of me getting the job is now much lower as other good candidates are on the list. If I don't get the job, there's no real future for me at Dart Water."

Antonia removed her hands. Frowning, she sat back. "Peter, what are you saying?"

"I want to be absolutely honest with you. If I'm not appointed to this role, then my career with the company is dead. The only way to progress is for me to find a senior job elsewhere, but that would be off the island – maybe back to Australia or the Middle East or somewhere else. I just don't know."

The colour drained from Antonia's face. She picked up her glass with shaking fingers and sipped the juice. Peter could see she couldn't speak, couldn't form thoughts in her mind. She stood up, grabbed her handbag and went to leave. Peter took her arm and asked her to stay for five minutes. She didn't agree or disagree; she was frozen in shock.

"Antonia, please sit down. Let's talk about this. I don't know yet that I won't get the job. Everything might go well for me."

Slowly, she sat down. She found her voice, quiet and flat, but she couldn't look at Peter. "And if it doesn't, you're quite happy to leave the island and leave me behind? I thought you loved me. Really loved me. I've been such a fool, I should have—"

"I do love you, so much I can't describe it. But I have to have a career and I hope so much that it will be here in Antigua with you."

"Yes, that's what I want, too. For you to be here. I have my own career to think about as well. If I was still with the airline, maybe I would join you wherever you went in the world, but I've just started my new life and my new job. I'm enjoying it so much, I don't want to give it up. It was a mistake getting so involved with you. We should call it off now. Nice knowing you, Peter." Tears welled in Antonia's eyes.

"No, please, Antonia, we should stay together. Wait to see if I get the job. And if I don't, I might well decide to stay here in my current role."

"And be unhappy all the time? You will come to resent me."

"If we love each other, surely we will always be happy together?"

"But don't you see?" Antonia's voice had recovered – she had found a new determination. "We've just established that we'd both put our careers ahead of our love for each other. What sort of relationship is that? No, we clearly don't have a future together. I should go. I wish you well." She stood quickly and pushed her chair in.

Peter made no effort to stop Antonia leaving. He knew it would be futile.

TWENTY-FOUR

In the weeks that followed, Antonia took refuge in her work. The height of the season was approaching, with fabulous sunny weather every day, settled seas and beautiful breezy evenings to enchant visitors. Regular meetings with hoteliers, the port staff and government officials gave her a strong sense of purpose and made each day pass quickly and smoothly. She also spent more time at the gym, started to socialise with the expats at the Mango Tree, and even took sailing lessons in the harbour and joined the sailing club. She took care to shop at the Gourmand during weekday mornings, confident that Peter would be at work and she wouldn't bump into him. She never went to Ffryes beach or Diana's; that would be too painful.

Antonia had confided in Florence that the relationship was over, but had not given a reason; that was personal to her and Peter. She simply said that the romance had run its course and it was time to move on. She couldn't bear to admit to Florence that she was deeply hurt by the separation, that she wanted to see Peter every day and that she yearned to hold him again. Florence was kind and supportive, offering a shoulder to cry on and saying that she was there if Antonia needed to talk.

She had thought about what to do if Peter contacted her; she was determined not to be drawn into seeing him again. But as he hadn't called or messaged, her resolve hadn't been tested. She also controlled her desire to contact him. She knew she had to suffer in silence until the pain faded, if it ever did. She was well practised in managing her emotions – lessons learned when her relationship with Steve had ended over two years ago.

With just two weeks until Christmas, preparations were being made at the office for the staff party. Antonia doubted that she would enjoy it, but she would attend anyway, partly because it was her duty as a manager, but it also meant one less evening spent at home on her own. She had agreed to video call her mother on Christmas Day, first thing in the morning Antigua time, so she'd catch her family before they sat down to dinner and the King's speech on television. She had texted her mother telling her about her break-up with Peter, but she kept it matter-of-fact. She didn't want to make a big deal of it.

Her previous job with the airline had meant she was often away at Christmas, so she didn't feel the urge that most people have to spend Christmas at home with family. Florence had invited Antonia to her house to join her and her mother for lunch on Christmas Day. She gladly accepted and had a lovely time. It lifted her spirits to a level she hadn't felt since the time before she and Peter had broken up.

The week of the new year saw the whole island bustling: three cruise ships came into St John's and every hotel and resort was full to capacity. Reports were coming in that tourists were spending their dollars freely and all the visitor sites were fully staffed. The island's economy was booming.

***

Antonia had not taken any time off for several months, so Florence encouraged her to think about having a break for two or three days. It made sense: all the tourism plans were in place and working well, and there were no crises to attend to nor any complaining tour operators, so why not?

Antonia started her break by spending the day with friends from the sailing club, helping to crew a thirty five foot sailing yacht on a trip down to English Harbour. After arrival, they had a late lunch at a restaurant looking out over the sea. She sat with a crew member, an American called Drake Sneider. She felt a kinship with him – not just for his sailing skills, but because her grandfather was also called Drake. She enjoyed his company and picked up vibes from him that he was keen on her, so didn't resist his advances. At the end of the lunch, he gave her a card with his phone number and said he would love to meet her for dinner some time. She was flattered; he was a very good-looking man, probably in his late forties, and had an engaging character.

On the return trip, they passed Darkwood and Ffryes. Although they were well out to sea, she could see Diana's bar and felt a familiar twang of regret. A call to tack distracted her and occupied her mind and body for several minutes as the yacht changed heading. When she looked back, they were alongside the next headland and she could see Sheer Rocks. Again, anguish tied her stomach in knots as she recalled the wonderful night she and Peter had spent there. She forced herself to look straight ahead and at the skipper, concentrating on listening to his instructions.

Arriving home after a couple of drinks and a light meal in the sailing club, she thought about what to do on her second day of holiday. She needed to do some housework and decided to set to it immediately, to leave the next day free. The box of papers Peter had pulled from the sea had rested untouched for several weeks on her coffee table. As she dusted around it, she had a thought. She decided to go into St John's and speak to the museum people the next day. She took out the papers and laid them flat in a plastic folder, then slid it into her tote bag.

***

For the first time in a long time, Antonia slept well. The sea air and the physical effort of crewing had done her good. She looked at the card Drake had given her and smiled. Maybe some time… After an early breakfast, she drove up to St John's. The town was quiet; a cruise ship had docked overnight, but it was too early for the mass of passengers to swarm out and flood the duty-free shops, gift shops and cafés of Heritage Quay.

"Good morning, how may I help you?" The assistant at the museum wore a white blouse under a dark blue trouser suit. Her name badge read 'Janelle'.

"I have some old papers here that I would like to show you and ask some questions." Antonia placed the file on the reception counter. "They seem to relate to the ownership of land down near Ffryes beach."

"Right, I can certainly ask one of my colleagues here to help you. If you take a seat at the desk over there, I will give her a call."

Sharon Dubois introduced herself as the deputy archivist, then sat down at the desk. After explaining that she had found the box and papers, Antonia said she was keen to know if the ownership deed was valid or if the land had been sold to someone else.

Sharon nodded politely as Antonia explained exactly where she had found the box, and how she had opened it and tried to make sense of the papers.

"It's highly unlikely that the sale of the land could be registered in England without the papers that certified ownership," said Sharon. "Around the time of the letter to the English solicitors, it was rare for duplicate papers to be made. As the originals were lost at sea, the records in England would still show the previous owner. If someone knew the box had fallen overboard – the new owner, for example – and they cared sufficiently to go through all the necessary proceedings, it might have been possible to have a new title of ownership drawn up. But it would have been a long, time-consuming process. It's highly likely that the new owner didn't know what had happened to the box or they just didn't bother. They might have relied on an informal document such as a sales receipt to prove ownership."

"I see, thank you," said Antonia. "I definitely feel confident that the deeds and other papers we have will be sufficient to have the property confirmed as being in the ownership of the same family, but I'm concerned that there might have been a sale at some time between 1892 and now. Finding those records is just as important."

Sharon nodded. "Quite so. But setting aside that possible sale, it means that since the loss of the papers back in 1892, and assuming no duplicates were created, nothing can now be done with the land. No building, commercial use or selling on. It seems to me that if and when it was discovered that the papers were lost, which could have been years later, by the way, valid duplicates could have been made up and held by the Land Registry department here on Antigua. Have you contacted them?"

"No, I didn't think of that. Sorry," said Antonia.

"No problem at all. It's not easy to navigate the records, but I can look up the register for you right now and see if they have any details on file."

"That would be brilliant, thank you."

Sharon logged on to the Land Registry website and, at a speed that astounded Antonia, worked her way through the portals and into the records for St Mary's parish, which included the Ffryes area. She looked gloomy as she patiently searched every possible option to find records of ownership of Ffryes Mills.

After nearly half an hour, she sat back in her chair and folded her arms. "Well, Antonia, I have to conclude that there are no records for the Ffryes Mills estate. And I cannot see any other registration for that area that might be relevant. But, you know, it's not so unusual in the Caribbean islands for ownership to be uncertain or disputed. Another angle might be for you to contact the firm of solicitors in England, if they still exist, to see if they hold any ownership papers – letters, duplicates of your papers, or any records of a sale since 1892."

"Good idea. I will look up firms of solicitors in Wells and see what I can turn up. You've been really helpful, Sharon, thank you so much."

"It's my pleasure. But one other thing. We have here in the museum a large selection of ownership documents, maps and plans of sugar estates. You would be welcome to look through them at any time. You might find some mention of Ffryes Mills."

"Great, thanks again." Antonia shook hands with Sharon and walked to the exit. Janelle smiled and waved her out of the door.

TWENTY-FIVE

Antonia decided that a third day of holiday would do her good and planned to continue working on the Ffryes Mills mystery. She realised that the next logical step in her enquiries was to go and see Ettie again. This worried her, as she would be involving herself with the personal life of the old lady. Antonia pondered how she could approach Ettie without seeming to be intrusive and without upsetting her. She didn't want to blunder into the windmill again. It was clear to Antonia that she should go and speak to Diana, and ask how she might get to talk to Ettie without alarming her.

However, that would, of course, involve going to Ffryes beach and into Diana's bar, reviving all the thoughts and emotions of her time with Peter. She sighed. If she wanted to pursue her interest in the history of this part of the island, she would just have to control her feelings. And she knew that she wanted to help Ettie and find her a more secure place to live, in one of the villages perhaps where the community would look after her.

So, after morning coffee, she packed her beach bag and drove down to Ffryes. As usual, the sun was shining, the water was crystal clear and the sand was so white and smooth that it was dazzling. Antonia had a short swim, then rested under a sunshade before dressing in her sarong, taking a deep breath and walking up the steps to Diana's. It was not quite lunchtime and the place was quiet. Diana was behind the bar, writing the day's specials on a small blackboard. Antonia waved and called over that she would take a table on the far side of the veranda.

"Great to see you again – it has been a while," said Diana as she handed Antonia a menu.

"Yes, I've been really busy at work; the Ministry of Tourism. I'm taking a few days off to recharge, and what better place than here at Ffryes?"

Diana laughed. "No better place! Your friend Peter comes regularly for evening drinks. In fact, he is guaranteed to be here when the conditions are right for a good sunset. He usually takes that table at the front."

Antonia stifled a gasp as Diana indicated the table where they had always sat to watch the sunset. "That's wonderful, but I haven't seen Peter for some time. In fact, after I've ordered, I was hoping to take a couple of minutes of your time to ask you a question…"

"Oh, right. Sure, that's fine. What would you like today?"

"I see you have a prawn and dill risotto on the specials board. I'd like that, please, and a mango and orange juice."

"Great choice. I'll take the food order to the kitchen and be right back."

Antonia sat back and consciously relaxed her shoulders, breathing slowly and steadily. Her fingers were shaking, but she knew she was doing well. She told herself she just needed to stay positive and think about Ettie, nothing else.

"What was it you wanted to ask?" said Diana, sitting down opposite Antonia.

"Well, do you remember that Peter and I met Ettie when we looked inside the windmill at the back of Ffryes? You mentioned then that she does some work here."

"Yes, that's right – five evenings a week, helping in the kitchen."

"The thing is, I've come across some papers dating from the 1890s that show the ownership of a piece of land called Ffryes Mills, in the name of a Nathaniel Foster. I'm trying to find out if the land was ever sold on or if the Foster descendants are still the owners."

"That's incredible. Ettie is always saying she comes from a wealthy family that owned a plantation, but no one takes her seriously. She is a touch eccentric, you know. It would be quite something if she could prove she was the owner of the land."

"Yes, that's what we, I mean, *I* thought. I'd like to talk to her, to understand her story, but I feel reluctant to just turn up at the windmill. I was hoping you could have a chat with her and ask if she would like to meet me."

"I would be delighted to. Why not come back tomorrow evening? She will be here then. Say around seven, before it gets too busy? I will reserve this table; it's nice and quiet."

"That would be brilliant. Thank you so much, Diana."

"No problem, but I'm curious about something. Where did you find the papers?"

"They were in an old document box that Peter and I found in the sea after the hurricane. I've discussed them with the museum in St John's."

"Right. There is one more thing I should say…"

"Oh yes?"

"Be aware that others have tried to get hold of the land over the last few years. I guess the problems with ownership have blocked any deals. But if there was a way to prove who the rightful owner is, and if the land could be developed for a hotel or something, it would be a very valuable piece of real estate."

TWENTY-SIX

Peter felt that the video meeting with the headhunters in Miami went well. Allowing for their American interviewing technique, a formulaic series of questions, he believed he had shown his scientific and technical knowledge, good strategic thinking, and evidence of his experience in people management. Frustrating though it was, he received no direct feedback after the interview. However, the next day, George came to find him and said, "Well done yesterday. Come and have coffee."

The changing global climate brought no positive news for the Caribbean states. The risk of more frequent and more severe hurricanes was matched with a trend for spells of intolerably hot weather well into the forties at times. The need for water was steadily increasing, for residents and visitors alike, and the planned expansion of the Dart Water Health plant was only the beginning. There would be a similar demand for growth at other plants and possibly even the need for new facilities to be built.

But Peter was struggling. He had never been the type of person to dismiss his concerns and carry on without a care in the world. His anguish at losing Antonia was eating into his sense of purpose in life. He tried to balance the pressures of work, including the promotion question, with getting out and enjoying himself or, at least, keeping busy and occupied. He went back to playing golf regularly and enjoyed swimming in the sea at Ffryes beach. The guys at the plant were as accommodating as ever, inviting him out for drinks, impromptu cricket matches and social events, like birthday barbecues and get-togethers for a few beers for no special reason.

After what seemed an interminable wait, the day of his interview came near, giving him a week in which to do some serious preparation. He had a nagging thought that he no longer wanted the job; that it might actually be a good thing if he had to go elsewhere in the world. That way, he would be better able to put Antonia out of his mind, rather than suffer the torment of being reminded of her everywhere he went. Why put all that effort into preparing for an interview for a job he didn't really want? But he couldn't deny that the job was something that he desired enormously, so he prepared for it and focused on giving the interview his best shot.

He searched the internet for information on desalination, reverse osmosis and water recycling from around the world. His research alerted him to greater efforts being made in natural water capture in reservoirs and holding tanks. He knew that many scientists and engineers took a biased approach to water conservation as a long-term solution, preferring their science-based treatment methods. He hoped he wasn't one of them; all the treatment processes involved huge amounts of electrical power and produced damaging saline waste products. Ultimately the best enviromental option was to conserve and use the island's rainfall.

The interview panel consisted of the chairman, the finance director, two non-executive directors and George Robartes. Peter was told to allow two hours for the meeting and was asked to prepare a twenty-minute presentation on the strategic direction that Antigua should take on the supply of water. This he was able to do without any difficulty, as he had been working on the very topic for the past six months as an aside to his main job at the plant.

The questioning was tough and in-depth. The directors wanted to hear his justification for his approach to the water supply. They also pressed him on financial management issues and challenged him on how he saw the long-term viability of the water supply to residents and businesses, without the support of subsidies from the government.

As the interview approached the two-hour mark, Peter detected the interview panel taking a softer line. The two non-executive directors sat back and exchanged whispers, then nodded and smiled. Did this mean he was doing well or were they agreeing that another candidate was better? The chairman turned his questioning to personal matters: how had Peter settled into island life? What were his ambitions in his career? George stayed silent during the closing phase of the interview, then the chairman thanked Peter for an excellent presentation and for providing his thoughts on the challenges of water supply for the islands.

***

In George's office, a tray stood waiting, holding a pot of coffee, cups and cold milk. George poured and offered Peter a piece of rum cake. Even though he had had his usual breakfast, Peter took the cake in order to be sociable.

"Yes, well done yesterday, Peter. The directors were very impressed."

"Thanks, George. I was pleased myself. I was certainly given ample opportunity to lay out my ideas and go through the strategic options for the plant. Can't have any complaints about that."

"No, I feel it all bodes well. But let's be realistic now. We have seen three candidates from the US, with two more to come, one of whom is the Antiguan national. At the moment, you are the best candidate, that's just between us. I know the panel will try to be impartial in their recommendation to the board, but we have to accept that the Antiguan candidate has an advantage over all the others. And he has an excellent CV."

"I can understand that. It's only natural," said Peter.

"However, as I have mentioned before, the choice of chief scientist will be communicated to the World Bank before the appointment is finalised. We need to be sure they are one hundred per cent happy and that our choice will support, not obstruct, our application for funding. Now, this is a personal view, but the board has to be doubly sure that the candidate is worthy of the role based on technical and managerial merit. They won't give it to him just because he is Antiguan. I'm sure you see the point I'm making here."

"I think I do. Maybe being an Antiguan could work against the candidate. I just hope that the board keep a level playing field. If he is a good scientist, right for the job, then his nationality shouldn't be an issue one way or another, any more than my British nationality is."

"OK, fine. I have another question, if I may. Don't think I'm prying into your personal affairs, but I have to ask as it's relevant to the job. In the interview, you didn't mention your girlfriend. If the board could see that you were settled here on the island, it could work to your advantage."

"Yes, I see that, but we are no longer together. The relationship came to an end a while ago. I hope that doesn't count against me with the panel?"

"No, no. No problem there, I was just hoping there might be a small point in your favour," said George. "Now, the board will make their decision within a week. I'll keep you informed as best I can during that time. In the meantime, I'm sure you will agree, we should just get back to work." George smiled.

"Agreed. There is certainly plenty to be getting on with, as the night-time processing will start at the beginning of next week."

TWENTY-SEVEN

Antonia arrived at Diana's with twenty minutes to spare, so she went for a walk along the beach. There was a blanket of thin, high cloud and a soft, shadowy sunset without the spectacular rays of red and gold sunlight she often saw. The sky was darkening quickly, so she strolled up to Diana's and took her seat at the reserved table. Within a few minutes, Diana came over.

"I'm afraid you might find Ettie reluctant to talk. She didn't want to meet you today – she's afraid you plan to remove her from the windmill, but I assured her that all you're interested in is island history. She will be out shortly."

"Thanks, Diana. I will take it slowly."

"OK. I'll bring over a jug of mango juice and a couple of glasses."

It was ten minutes before Diana reappeared with the drinks and with Ettie by her side. Antonia stood and held out her hand, smiling. Ettie took her hand, said a simple, "Evenin'," and sat down. She was dressed in an immaculately starched white linen kitchen jacket and trousers with mid-blue rubber sandals. She looked clean and her hair was well groomed. Antonia guessed that Diana had helped Ettie prepare, allowing her to use the staff shower and changing room.

"Nice to see you again, Ettie. Do you remember me? I'm afraid I stumbled uninvited into your windmill. I apologise again for being so clumsy."

"Yes, ma'am, I remember. You were with a man. Where is he now?"

"Ah well, we are no longer close friends. It's just me who wanted to meet you. I hope to understand more about the history of Antigua and – if you can tell me – your own life story."

"I can tell you sometin' about the island, but you won't believe me when I tell you about my family. Nobody does."

"Have you always lived in this area? Around Ffryes, I mean?"

Ettie sat back with her eyes half closed and a frown between her eyes, in a show of making an effort to recollect times past. "No. I grew up in the village of Bolans, you know it?" Ettie didn't wait for a reply. "I had a little schoolin' and then worked with my mother doin' her beachcombin'. Bolans was a nice friendly little place, on the way to St John's, but hotel and housebuilding changed all that. My house was hit by a hurricane six years ago and so I moved to my windmill. That's not goin' nowhere in a hurricane."

Ettie laughed to herself.

"A lot of people make a few dollars findin' nice shells and stones on the beach for the jewellers who make the earrings, bracelets and necklaces to sell to tourists. We used to come here and Darkwood sometimes to do our shell findin'. Mother was a good, hard-workin' woman, but it was Father who ran the family. I had two older sisters. They got jobs in English Harbour restaurants and soon they marry and live down there. They not with us anymore."

"Diana told me that you believe you own the windmill and maybe the land. Is that right?" said Antonia.

"Sure t'ing. Father, when he had a rum or two, he would say he hoped one day to reclaim the family's land here at Ffryes Mill. It was promised to him by his father, who said that his father had bought the land way back in time from the English owner. What happen is, Great-grandfather was working at another sugar mill up in the hills owned by the same man when a fire broke out in the mill. Great-grandfather went back in to save the plantation owner's son. He was so grateful, he sold the Ffryes Mills land and windmill to Great-grandfather for just a pound. But nobody knew that, so, later, when my grandfather went to the government people to get them to make a new deed of ownership, they laughed at him and sent him away. My father do the same, get the same treatment. Now I'm the last of the family and no one respects me as the rightful owner."

"Did you ever marry, Ettie?" Antonia asked in a low voice. She needed to know if there was a husband around who might also have a strong interest in the ownership of the land.

"No, ma'am. One boy came to see me a few times and we swam together, walk hand in hand along Ffryes, watched the sunsets, drink mango juice."

Antonia could easily see the couple in her mind.

"But he more interested in the land and when he hear there was no proof of ownership, him disappear quick. No, missy, no one interested in a girl who everyone calls Mad Ettie."

Antonia sat back, thrilled but also saddened at the story. She could hardly contain her excitement at realising that she might well be able to confirm that Nathaniel Foster, and consequently Ettie, owned the land. But this was not the time to mention the box and the papers; she knew she had to take things carefully, not get Ettie's hopes up, only to find the land had been legitimately sold to someone else after 1892. It would take much more investigation to establish an unbroken link. Still, Antonia was inspired by Ettie's story and was determined to do the best she could to establish the true picture.

"Do you like working here, Ettie?"

"Sure me do. Diana's a nice lady and she pays me well. Her family also from Bolans way."

"I didn't know that. It's good to have a job, to make some money."

"Yes, she kind lady. She pays me and feeds me, like a daughter I never have." Ettie was gazing out to sea and Antonia knew it was time to end the discussion – for now at least.

After Ettie had returned to the kitchen, Diana came over.

"Thanks for arranging that, Diana. It was very interesting," said Antonia. "She mentioned you were from the same village, Bolans."

"That's right. I now live with my husband and family in St John's."

"But did you know Ettie's family when you lived there?"

"Sure, my parents were friends with her parents and older sisters. We all knew the family's belief that they were landowners. I guess that's the reason I look out for Ettie – no one else will and I feel it's right to help your old neighbours if you can."

Antonia was touched. "That's so kind of you, Diana."

"Not really. She works well and we need staff."

Antonia felt that Diana was being modest and self-effacing, but she didn't linger on the subject.

"But surely there must be somewhere else she could live that's more secure and comfortable?" said Antonia.

"Ettie lives there because she believes that if she abandoned the property, she would always be denied ownership."

"Right, I see. I didn't mention the papers I found; there is more work to be done to verify the ownership of the land. But it would be wonderful if it could be proved that she owns Ffryes Mill, don't you think?" said Antonia.

"It certainly would. But as I've mentioned, there are many people who would like to disprove her ownership and get hold of the land. Many have tried and failed, because of the lack of ownership papers."

Diana went back to her work as the restaurant was getting busy. Antonia suddenly thought she might see Peter if he came in for drinks or dinner. She left a few dollars for the drinks and walked back to her car.

***

That evening, Antonia searched the internet for firms of solicitors in Wells. There were many to choose from, but only one firm mentioned a long history, going back to 1870. Although its name was not 'Carter, Kingsnorth' but 'Cathedral Law', Antonia wondered if perhaps it was the same firm and its name had changed over time. It was as good a place to start as any and she began to draft an email, asking if they had ever acted for Ffryes Mills.

It didn't take long to write. Antonia sat back and looked at the draft, saved it and asked herself why she was doing this work. What might she stir up and would it end happily or result in more stress for Ettie – and indeed for herself? At work, her fascination with Antiguan history as a basis for developing tourism ideas had fallen on deaf ears, so she needed to make sure she kept her interest in the island's history personal. Only the staff at the museum, Diana, Peter and Florence knew about the box and the papers, and none of them knew the whole story. She decided not to discuss it with anyone else.

***

In the morning, Antonia looked again at her draft email.

enquiries@cathedrallawwells.co.uk

Hello,

I wonder if you can help me. I believe that your firm may be the successors to a firm of solicitors called Carter, Kingsnorth, dating back to the 1890s. First, may I ask if this is correct?

My enquiry relates to title deeds and other papers in regard to a sugar plantation, originally named Ffryes Mills, on the island of Antigua in the West Indies. I am acting for a friend who's interested in verifying the ownership of the estate, which was sold in around 1892.

If you hold any relevant records, I would very much welcome a video call to discuss the details.

I will, of course, be happy to pay for this work.

Many thanks

Antonia Casey-Brown

Jolly Harbour,

Antigua and Barbuda, WI.

The comment about acting for a friend was only a white lie. She decided not to mention that she had the box and the papers. She wanted the solicitors to investigate their archives and see what they could turn up.

She pressed send.

TWENTY-EIGHT

Peter had become resigned to the outcome of the interview process to the point of nonchalance – he said to himself that it would be what it would be and he had done everything he reasonably could to be offered the chief scientist job. There was no need to worry now or even think about the role. George had told him quietly that he was one of two on the final shortlist and it was now up to the chairman and non-executive directors to choose who they would put forward to the board. Just like everything else related to island life, it would take time, possibly a couple of weeks, for the recommendation to be made and the board to make their decision.

But as the time got nearer, his thoughts turned regularly to Antonia. He was baffled and hugely saddened by their separation. After George had advised him about the shortlist, Peter decided to go and have a drink after work at Diana's. He told himself it was a treat; he had done well to get to the last two. But as he sat at the table at the front of the terrace, he knew he had come here with the hope of seeing Antonia; a chance meeting would allow him to talk to her, to try to rekindle her love. He didn't want to call or text her and ask her to meet: what if she refused?

The bar was getting busy with tourists and locals. Peter glanced round and saw what looked like a couple of businessmen arrive, one in dark blue trousers and white shirt and the other in pink shorts and a garish Caribbean shirt. They sat at the table just behind him. He thought that he vaguely recognised the man in the white shirt, but then realised it could be any one of the businessmen or government people he met through work.

The sun had set. Unusually, the night was cloudy, moonless and starless. The dinner service was well underway. Peter ordered a spicy grilled steak, fries and a salad, and another Wadadli beer. Although the bar was full, with guests happily chatting and laughing, he couldn't help overhearing some of the discussion with the two men. They seemed to be talking about new hotels and resorts on the island. Peter risked a glance over his shoulder at the familiar man. When he saw him again and heard his voice, it clicked – it was Antonia's boss, Aaron Jaygo, who he had met on the boat trip. *Nothing very exciting*, he thought. *Just the tourism hierarchy planning money-spinning activities.* Peter focused on the lights in the villas at the far end of the beach, the beautiful Tamarind Hills development. He knew that as well as the holiday lets, a number of people lived there permanently and he had to confess to himself that it would be a dream location to set up home. Or it would be if he had someone to share the life with him.

The two men behind him were talking more loudly, drawing his attention away from his thoughts of an idyllic home and relationship. He tuned in.

"No, no, no, Aaron, you can trust me on this! We will have the old lady removed, taken to a nice, secure apartment in a good rest home, and no one will hear her silly stories again. We will still have the problem of ownership papers, but when we have the authenticated copies of the 1880 sale from the UK, then we will be in a position to get the final papers we need from the US. I have the architect's plans for the hotel, all ready for the construction company."

"I can't say I'm happy with this, Ethan." Aaron wrung his hands and looked closely at his friend. "Kidnapping is a serious offence."

"Such a suggestion!" Ethan laughed loudly. "It's a happy relocation – with her permission, of course, to where the lady will be properly fed and cared for. Funded by my company, with a pension to meet her costs for as long as she lives. You can be assured of that. Just help us get the ownership papers sorted out and your part in the project will be complete. And look at the wonderful service you will do your country."

"OK, OK. Our lawyers are in touch with the British solicitors in Wells and are expecting copies of the title deeds within two weeks. A courier will be flying over with them."

"Excellent, Aaron. Deliver them to my office as soon as they arrive, please. I will then have my lawyers check them out and… supply any other necessary documents."

"What do you mean, 'supply'?"

"The Land Registry people may well require other papers. We want things to be complete, don't we?" said Ethan.

This time, it was Aaron who raised his voice. "I will have nothing to do with anything underhand. No forgeries are to be made from the papers that are sent over from England!"

"Relax, Aaron. So long as we can take good, clear documents to the government offices to get the land registered in my company's name, all will be well."

The waitress came to Peter's table to remove the plates and glasses. Peter ordered coffee; he didn't want to leave just yet.

"And compensation for your time and special services will be paid into your bank account."

"You know I'm not doing this for the money, Ethan. It's what's best for Antigua; that's where my interests lie. We need to be developing our coastal assets with the most desirable hotels and destinations."

"Absolutely, but the ten thousand US will cover your expenses," Ethan sneered. "A minor amount in the grand scheme of things."

A group of six American tourists came and sat at a nearby table, loud and merry. Peter could hear no more of the discussion between Aaron Jaygo and Ethan. He paid his bill and walked quickly back to his house, confused and unsure about what he should do.

TWENTY-NINE

The best part of a week had gone by and Peter had not contacted Antonia about the conversation he had overheard. Although he knew she was interested in the Ffryes Mills papers and the woman who lived in the windmill, Peter was afraid that she'd see this as a weak excuse to contact her. As Peter arrived at work on Wednesday morning, he still felt confused. He just didn't know what to do for the best. As he walked into the office, he saw George Robartes and the chairman already there and he was jolted out of his thoughts. They invited him into the boardroom.

George poured three coffees and they made small talk about the hot weather, the prospect of rainfall later in the week to help with the fresh water supply and the absence of Category 5 hurricanes for the time of year.

"Take a seat, Peter. We have some news for you," said George.

Peter took a deep breath. He guessed he was going to be given the outcome of the selection process. "Thanks, George. Chairman."

"But first I want to tell you how difficult it has been to select our new chief scientist," the chairman said. "We had several excellent candidates, each with their own advantages. The feedback I have collated from all the interviewers has been unanimous, however, helping us to make our decision for the way forward, although these things can never be entirely objective, can they?"

George coughed gently and looked sideways at the chairman, who looked back to Peter. "I'm sure you would like me to get straight to the point."

"Yes, I would indeed."

"Well, after careful consideration, the board has made its decision," said the chairman. He hesitated. "I'm afraid I have to tell you that you have not been selected for the role. The position has been offered to our Antiguan candidate, who will be returning to the island after six years of working in the United States. We need his technical experience to ensure that the improvements we need at Ffryes go ahead."

Peter felt an immediate sense of frustration, but knew he had to control his emotions. "I see. I understand, Chairman. I'm sure he will be a great chief scientist."

George spoke up. "Yes, we are all confident of that, but the chairman has some other news he would like to give you. Chairman?"

"Thank you, George. Yes. Now, Peter, as well as the plant here at Ffryes, you know that we have water production sites across the island. With the greater demand for water, we want to extend our island-wide approach to all the supply options available to us, including filtration, storage and so on. So we wish to appoint a director of water strategy at the Ministry of Utilities and we would like to offer you the job. In effect, this is a promotion above the level of chief scientist. The role will be based in the government offices in St John's and you would be provided with an apartment in the city."

Peter was astounded. "Really? That would be excellent – absolutely the kind of work I'd like to do."

"We hoped that would be the case. We admire your scientific knowledge, Peter, but it's in the strategic management of water resources where we feel you would best serve the islands and, of course, develop your career over the long term. Take a minute or two to look at this." The chairman passed over a contract. "Can I take it you are willing to accept the job, after you have read the full contract?"

Peter scanned the document. "Most certainly!" He was about to receive a forty per cent salary increase and a package of government-related benefits.

The chairman stood and held out his hand. "Congratulations, Peter. I wish you a long and successful career here in Antigua."

"And let me add my own congratulations." George shook Peter's hand warmly.

"Thank you, thanks so much. I will really look forward to the new job."

Peter returned to his desk and read the contract carefully. He found it all in good shape and he noticed that he would be moving up to St John's in less than a month. He was delighted with the outcome of the interviews; he hadn't dared to hope for this so early in his career. Excited, he picked up his phone and started to tap out a text. He wanted to let Antonia know his news straight away. He ignored the nagging doubt that she wouldn't want to hear from him – surely she would be pleased for him? – and composed the message. He finished by asking her to meet him for drinks that evening at Jolly Harbour.

But then a sudden thought hit him and he stopped dead. Did he really think Antonia would welcome him with open arms, now that he had sorted his job out? No, of course she wouldn't; it was stupid of him to think she might. He deleted the message and turned to study the spreadsheets and reports on his desk.

THIRTY

Antonia was astonished when she received an email the next day from Merryn Penrose, the commercial partner of Cathedral Law, confirming that all matters relating to Carter, Kingsnorth were now being handled by Cathedral Law. It was a standard reply to any enquiry. But below this was a more interesting paragraph. It said she would be very happy to schedule a video call: would 9 a.m. Antigua time on the following Monday be convenient? Curiously, the message ended by saying, 'We are able to act with all haste on the matter if required'. *Very efficient*, Antonia thought. She had not said that her enquiry was urgent.

The day and time suited Antonia very well, as she would have the weekend to prepare for the call. She tended to work at home on Monday mornings, which was helpful; it would be impossible to keep the video call confidential in the Ministry of Tourism's open-plan office. Over the weekend, Antonia took out the papers and carefully read as much as she could of the fine, closely spaced handwriting. She felt she had a good mental picture of the estate and its business, so she went to bed on Sunday evening excited and intrigued about what she might hear the next day.

***

Without needing an alarm, Antonia was up and showered by 7 a.m. and opened a window. Outside, the marina was already bustling and it was a perfect Caribbean January day. She strolled down to the Gourmand for some fresh milk, fruit and croissants, then spent some time working. She made sure her laptop was on charge. A few minutes after nine, the call came through. She clicked to accept it and was greeted by a solicitor who Antonia considered to be remarkably young for a partner in a law firm. She looked to be under thirty-five.

"Good morning, Miss Casey-Brown. I'm Merryn Penrose. How are you today?"

"Very well, thank you, and you?"

"Fine, thank you. I have some papers here to assist us in looking at the ownership of Ffryes Mills, but I should say that without the written authority of the owner, I cannot divulge any information that is not in the public domain or is available to anyone through the usual search routes. Having said this, I hope to answer your questions."

"That's great. Thank you, Miss Penrose."

"Call me Merryn, please."

"Sure. And I'm Antonia."

"Great. Now, how can I help?"

"A friend of mine, living here on Antigua, whose name is Henrietta Foster, is having difficulty in proving that she is the rightful owner of the Ffryes Mills estate. Until the ownership is proven, I cannot provide a letter from the owner, of course. My friend Henrietta – we call her Ettie – inherited the property through her father some time ago. The Foster family apparently bought the property in the 1890s. Ettie is a frail old lady and finds all the legal paperwork confusing; I'm sure you know how it is. My aim is to clear up the ownership question once and for all, by proving that the property has remained in her family since that time and has never been sold on, so she still owns it. I hope you have all the records there."

"Well, we have a large collection of papers from the estate, but I think I should clarify how we see the ownership from our records. It's not just a question of whether the property has been sold on since the 1890s, but also what took place before then. Our records show that the last time the estate was sold was in 1880. It was purchased by our predecessor firm's client, Mr Arthur Arkwright, from one Elizabeth Harper: it appears that Mr Arkwright lived both here in Wells and in Antigua. We have no other papers registering a sale of Ffryes Mills to anyone and I can't recall any correspondence with a party named Foster. The position seems to be that Mr Arkwright's family line came to an end and no inheritance records can be traced. I fear that your friend may have great difficulty proving she has ownership."

"I see…" Antonia knew she had to make a quick decision. Should she keep the finding of the box and the papers proving the 1892 sale a secret or should she tell the solicitor everything?

Fortunately, Merryn spoke while Antonia was considering what to do. "Let me ask: is your friend, believing that she owns the property, planning to sell it on? The reason I ask is that there are other parties looking at this land and who owns it. They are making public enquiries so I am not breaching any confidentiality when I mention this. My firm will be providing validated copies of the 1880 sale to them."

This stunned Antonia. Who the hell could be making enquiries? Could it be Peter, Florence or Diana? They were the only people to know about the box and the papers found on the beach, other than the museum staff – and she immediately discounted them. But she quickly dismissed the idea that any of her friends would be doing anything behind her back – why would they get involved? But this news made up her mind. She resolved not to mention the papers to Merryn Penrose.

"No, no, it's nothing like that," Antonia said quickly. "People have wanted to develop the land in the past, but the ownership question has always got in the way. My friend simply wants to be able to confirm her ownership so she can live in peace on the land, perhaps build a new house there. But may I ask, who is making enquires?"

"Ah, that is confidential. Our solicitor/client relationship prevents me from disclosing their identity. The individuals are being represented by a firm of solicitors in St John's. The matter has been described as urgent: we have been asked to provide authenticated copies of the 1880 deeds within the next week or so."

"I see. Well, you have been very helpful, Merryn. Please send me your invoice whenever you're ready."

"Thank you. There is something else I should mention. If there was indeed a sale after 1880, a record of it could be with the Antiguan Land Registry. This was established in 1975. When it was set up, many people took the opportunity to file their ownership with them. So, for example, documents recording a sale at any time after the 1880 purchase by Arthur Arkwright's estate might well be registered in St John's."

"Thanks for mentioning that, Merryn, but I have made some enquiries already at the national museum and they kindly looked up the Land Registry records. There was nothing there."

"Really?" said Merryn. "That's strange. Perhaps it's worth checking to see if they have any papers at all in the names of Arkwright or Foster?"

"That's a good idea. I'll go back to them. In the meantime, thanks again for your help."

"My pleasure. Have a good day."

Merryn clicked on 'leave meeting' and the laptop reverted to showing the home screen.

THIRTY-ONE

Peter spent a quiet Sunday afternoon contemplating what to do. On the one hand, he felt a degree of reluctant self-satisfaction that he had not been the first to break; he had not got in touch with Antonia. While he missed her so much, he had learned to divert his thoughts to almost anything else. And she had not contacted him, from which he took no comfort. If he was honest with himself, he wanted to see her again. More than that, he wanted to be her partner again. But, of course, he now knew that he had a secure job on the island that he would relish and that would challenge him. Should he contact her, explain about the job, attempt to gauge her feelings? Try to convince her that he loved her so much that he'd always planned to get in touch and ask her to reconsider their relationship? His mind was tangled with all his thoughts and he needed to get out of the house for a walk to help him think straight.

After slowly strolling along Ffryes beach three times, he decided not to stay for the sunset and turned towards his house. Unconsciously, his pace picked up, despite the effort required in the heat of the late afternoon. He thought of nothing other than what he had to do. His inner self had taken over and made a decision. It was subconscious; he didn't need to analyse the pros and cons or be logical. All he had to do was be true to himself, act honestly and do what his heart directed him to do. He would phone Antonia as soon as he got home.

Peter guessed she would be preparing her evening meal; it was nearly six o'clock. He took a deep breath, then another, as he tapped in her number. But the phone just rang out, then went to voicemail. Peter hung up. Had she seen it was his number and ignored his call? Perhaps he should drive up and see her? She wouldn't refuse to let him into the apartment, surely? No, that would really look pushy; he would try her phone a second time. Again, it went to voicemail. This time, he left a message: 'Hi Antonia, it's me. I hope you're well. I hope it's OK to contact you. I just wanted to have a chat, maybe meet up, I've got something to tell you. I'm sorry I haven't been in touch for a while, but if you're free this evening I could drive up to Jolly Harbour. We could meet at the Mango Tree or I could come to your flat. Anyway, let me know. It's Sunday evening, by the way, about six o'clock. Thanks.'

Having made the call, Peter felt relaxed and happy. His nerves and fears had dissipated. He had gone with his true feelings and taken the step that he knew he had to. He held no resentment for Antonia; he understood that she would be very reluctant to call him – after all, it had been he who had raised the question over their future together with his job situation. If she were to ignore him and never call back or want to see him, at least he would know that he had tried. He even recovered something of an appetite and thought about going over to Diana's for dinner, but then felt it would be difficult to talk on the phone in the busy restaurant if Antonia called him back. He took a pizza out of the freezer and a bottle of Wadadli from the fridge, sat at his desk and opened a work file on his laptop.

***

Antonia was exhausted. After a full day out on the sailing club's yacht and a couple of drinks in the bar, she was looking forward to a quiet night in. Drake had been on the boat, but didn't join the rest of the crew for drinks; someone said he was meeting his girlfriend, which had made Antonia smile, glad that she hadn't accepted his invitation to go on a date. She stopped off at the storage room on the ground floor of the apartments to put away her waterproof jacket, deck shoes, hat, gloves and life jacket. Wearily, she slung her watertight dry bag over her shoulder and climbed the stairs to the first floor and opened her door. Antonia heard her phone buzzing in the bottom of her bag, but didn't rush to open it up and find the phone. She would check her messages later. She needed to shower, wash the salt from her hair, change into some comfortable clothes and make something to eat.

Feeling revived, and glowing after being in the sunlight all day, Antonia sat down after dinner with a small coffee and an even smaller glass of rum. She had a busy week at work ahead and didn't want to risk a headache in the morning. She pulled a large bean bag across in front of her and put her feet up. Then she looked at the screen of her mobile and saw she had one voice message. She pressed button three.

She listened to the message, then sat in shocked stillness. Tucked away in the back of her mind, she had the notion, or perhaps the wish, that Peter would contact her at some point. She couldn't decide if she felt fear or hope as she played the message again, and then for a third time, to make sure she understood exactly what he was saying, but more importantly to her, to take in his tone of voice and the emotions behind the message. He sounded unsure and nervous. *Not surprising, really*, Antonia thought. She looked at her watch. It had just gone seven o'clock. If she agreed to meet him now, would he think she was too keen? But she wanted to see him and find out what he wanted to tell her, so she called his number and waited, breathing deeply.

Peter picked up after just three rings.

"Hi, Peter, it's Antonia."

"Hi, great to hear from you. How are you doing?"

"Not bad, thanks. Pretty tired. I've been out with the sailing club all day. How are you?"

"I'm fine, thank you."

"Right, good," Antonia said slowly. "You mentioned in your voicemail there was something you wanted to say…"

"I did. Could I come up to your flat for an hour this evening? Or maybe we could meet at the Mango Tree?"

Antonia didn't feel like going out again. "Why don't you come here? Will you be leaving straight away?"

"Sure. I can be with you in about twenty minutes."

"Right, see you then."

Antonia whisked around the apartment, tidying the living room, putting her clothes and towels in the laundry. She put on shorts and a T-shirt, brushed her hair, tied it back in a ponytail and put on a little make-up. Right on time, there was a knock at the door. Antonia's heart fluttered and butterflies danced in her stomach.

"Hi. Come in." Antonia was thrilled to see Peter again. He leant forward to greet her, but with no more warmth than you would show brushing cheeks with a good friend.

"Thanks for seeing me at such short notice."

"No problem. Can I get you a drink? There's a beer in the fridge."

"Yes, that would be great, thanks." Peter followed Antonia into the kitchen. "How was the sailing?"

"Really good. We went out to Five Islands Bay. I think I'm getting the hang of crewing at last. It's hard work but fun. What about you? What have you been up to?"

"Golf up at Cedar Hills most weekends. Some cricket, swimming at Ffryes. You know how it is."

"Sounds good." After a few moments of silence, she said, "But you didn't come over to exchange sporting stories."

"No. I wanted to update you on work."

"Oh, right. Good news for you, I hope." Antonia opened the fridge and took out the beer and a can of cola, which she added to her rum. She took a sip and leant back against the kitchen counter.

"Yes and no, but mainly good news." Peter took a deep breath. "You know I applied for the chief scientist role? Well, I didn't get that job."

"Oh, Peter, I'm so sorry…"

Peter held up his hand. "No, no. It's no problem, really. I'm very happy because I have been offered something better – Director of Water Strategy for the whole island and Barbuda as well. I will be based in St John's, that's where the office is, and I'm being given a company flat there. I start next week."

Antonia laughed. "That's excellent. Congratulations!" She placed her glass on the work surface, stepped across the kitchen and hugged Peter. He hugged her back, but seemed reluctant, she thought, so she released him.

"Thanks. I'm really happy with the job and, of course, it means I will stay on Antigua for the foreseeable future."

Antonia simply said, "Mmm."

"I'm not saying that means that we're back on, I wouldn't be so presumptuous, but I have missed you hugely and want to see you again, if you are willing?" said Peter.

"Let's go through to the living room and sit down." Antonia took the single chair near the main door, leaving Peter the two-seater. "This news doesn't change things, does it? You were willing to leave me here in Antigua and go off somewhere else. Sure, I had to think about my job, too, but you didn't even ask me if I'd be willing to move away with you."

"I know. I just assumed you wouldn't want to. That was wrong of me. I'm sorry I was so short-sighted. I've had a long time to think over why we split up, but I see things so much more clearly now. Antonia, I want to spend as much time with you as I can. I still love you just as much as ever. There, I've said it! It's no good me trying to bottle up my feelings."

Peter's voice cracked and he suddenly stood up, strode across to the window and looked out across the harbour. With his back to Antonia, he couldn't see that she was close to tears of happiness and barely able to speak. But she managed to take a shaky breath.

"Are you sure? Is our relationship so important to you?"

Peter spun round to face her. "Of course it is! Please, let's get back to where we were. I really hope that's what you want."

"It is. I do want to be with you, always." Antonia stood up and they hugged long and passionately. "I've really missed you. I wanted to call, but I was worried that you wouldn't want to hear from me."

Peter touched her face. "How crazy have I been? I should have got back to you sooner, not wait for something like my job to kick me into action."

"It really is great that you have this new job – not just because it keeps you on the island, but for your career in the long term. You will become a world leader in water production!"

Peter laughed and stroked the hair back from Antonia's face, then ran his fingers down her neck. She purred gently and they kissed again.

"We must always talk openly to each other, Peter, don't let any secrets get between us. If anything ever troubles you, promise me you will tell me about it and we will sort things out."

Peter dabbed a tear from Antonia's cheek with his fingertip. "I will and you must do the same. Come on, let's sit down." Peter noticed the metal box he had pulled out of the sea sitting on the small coffee table. He pushed it aside to make room for his glass, then leant down and opened the lid, touched the papers and shut the lid again.

"You remember the box? I've been doing some research into the ownership of Ffryes Mills," said Antonia. "I've been in touch with the firm of solicitors in England that hold the historical papers for the estate."

Peter suddenly sat up straight, remembering the conversation he had overheard. He took Antonia's hands. "My love! I've just remembered, I've got something to tell you about Ffryes you're never going to believe!"

Antonia burst into laughter at Peter's sudden eagerness. "Come on, then – spill the beans!"

It was almost midnight when Peter left Antonia's apartment. They had passed the evening reading the papers and talking about how they had spent the time they had been apart. Antonia made plenty of coffee and warmed up some slices of Antiguan pecan and rum pie. When Peter described the conversation he had overheard between Aaron Jaygo and Ethan, Antonia gasped with surprise. They had to be the people who were requesting information from Cathedral Law. Antonia explained her conversation with Merryn Penrose and how the solicitor had mentioned the other enquiries being made. Antonia often saw people arriving at the office for meetings with Aaron, including several Americans, but couldn't think of someone called Ethan. She would be on the lookout for him from now on.

Peter then asked Antonia if she had any idea what the men were going to do with the copies of the ownership deeds and papers when they arrived from England. She said she needed to speak to Merryn again.

THIRTY-TWO

When Peter woke the next morning, he replayed the Ffryes discussions in his mind, but felt he had a more important thought to consider: their relationship. Peter had told Antonia he loved her, but he had not been overly passionate. He wondered if he had really seen her to persuade her to reconcile or if he had just wanted to share his excitement at his new job. No, he decided, he was perfectly happy with his motives. He'd talked of his love for her, several times, and he hoped she knew that he really did love her.

They had stayed in the living room, not taking the closeness they enjoyed through the evening into the bedroom. Peter didn't feel it would be the right thing to do. They needed to be sure of their newly rekindled relationship – they had not seen each other for several weeks and he wanted to take things slowly. He nodded towards the bedroom door and said, "Maybe not tonight?"

"No, that's fine." Antonia stroked Peter's cheek and hugged him firmly.

When he left, they agreed they'd meet again, as soon as Antonia had more information about Ffryes Mills. *The Ffryes affair seems to be the most important thing to Antonia*, Peter thought.

***

Antonia was further motivated to set up a video call with Merryn as this would hurry along her next meeting with Peter. The time difference would work to her advantage; she messaged Merryn to arrange the call for Wednesday, just two days away, at 7.30 a.m. Antigua time. She would still be in the office by 8.30 a.m.

Antonia had decided to tell Merryn about the papers in the box. She would also explain about the fire that Ettie had mentioned, and say why the mill had been sold to Nathaniel Foster, then ask if any details of this existed in the papers the law firm held. There must be a record of the intention to sell the land at the price Arthur Arkwright was willing to accept – amounting to giving away the land as a thank you for rescuing his son. But she wanted to make sure that if she told Merryn about these details, she would keep them confidential. She just had to put her trust in Merryn Penrose.

Antonia was up and prepared for the call ahead of time. She sat with her coffee in excited anticipation of making significant progress on the ownership of Ffryes Mills. At one minute past 7.30 a.m., the video call came through.

"Good morning, Antonia. How are you today?"

"Very well, thanks, Merryn. How about you?"

"Yes, fine thanks. How can I help?"

"I wanted to give you some further information on Ffryes, but before I do I need to ask you about confidentiality."

"Go on."

"If I share the details with you, can I be assured that you will not pass the information on to your other client? It is in regard to the question of ownership."

"I see," said Merryn, slowly and thoughtfully. "Have you acquired the information through your own research or is it information that would be available to anyone that took the trouble to look for it?"

"No, the information is in original papers that only I have."

"Right. Under those circumstances, I have no obligation to pass on the details to any other party without your permission. And more than that, I can undertake not to tell anyone that the information in regard to ownership even exists and is in your possession."

"That's great. Thank you." Antonia sat back, picked up the box, held it in front of the screen so Merryn could see it and took out a letter. "The information I have is detailed in this set of original documents relating to the sale of the property in 1892 by Arthur Arkwright to a Nathaniel Foster. The sale price was only one pound. This is a letter to Carter, Kingsnorth confirming it and there is a copy of the deed."

"That's amazing. Can I ask where you got these documents?"

"A friend of mine and I found the deed box washed up on the beach at Ffryes about five months ago. By a strange coincidence, we also met Ettie, the old lady who believes she is the rightful owner of the property. I described her as my friend, but I have to admit we really don't know each other well. Her name is Henrietta Foster, as I said. I have kept the existence of the documents secret, as we are still looking into how we can legally verify that Ettie is the current owner. She's the great-granddaughter of Nathaniel Foster. I haven't even mentioned the papers to her, but this can't go on for much longer. I feel that once the papers I have are confirmed as genuine, we can tell Ettie and she can take matters forward."

"That's incredible, Antonia, quite a find," said Merryn. "But when you're trying to prove that the papers are original and genuine, you may need supporting evidence. Have you found any other records that would attest to the ownership?"

"Unfortunately not. The only other source of information we have is Ettie herself. She maintains that the land was sold to her relative for a pound because there was a fire at another plantation Arkwright owned and Nathaniel Foster rescued Arkwright's son from the fire. To show his gratitude, Arkwright gave Foster the relatively small Ffryes plantation, with its windmill and equipment, all for one pound."

Merryn suddenly laughed out loud to Antonia's surprise – and consternation. "That's amazing. I have some letters in the file that we have been unable to make much sense of and they refer to a fire. One mentioned that an estate overseer had heroically gone back into the building and carried out Henry Arkwright, the son of the owner. This corroborates your story, but, as far as I know, there are no records of the sale. That, of course, could be because the papers had not yet been received from Antigua. And it wouldn't have been unusual for all the affairs of an estate owned by an Antiguan to have been managed locally, so no further documents, ledgers, accounts and so on would have been sent to England. So the question arises, are there any records in Antigua?"

"I'm still making enquiries. In the meantime, thank you, Merryn, that's really helpful. It's brilliant that you have a record of the fire. I think I will have to go and see Ettie and tell her what I have learned, and show her the deed box and the documents. I will also go back to the museum to look again at their records."

"Yes, that makes sense. And let me know if I can be of any further help."

"Will do. I'll be in touch. If anything develops with the other party, would you be kind enough to let me know? Within the bounds of client confidentiality, of course."

"Um… yes, that shouldn't be a problem."

THIRTY-THREE

Peter was happy that he had got in touch with Antonia and was so pleased that she had taken him back into her life. He knew she would be wary, would need reassuring that he truly did adore her. He felt lucky; she might well have rejected him for having caused her so much anguish. However, he had to do more than just say the words; he had to demonstrate his love for her and his commitment. In future, he would be much more selfless when it came to thinking of their relationship and how they would build their lives together. His feelings for Antonia were so different to his feelings for Stephanie, his previous girlfriend. His love for Antonia was deep, elemental, essential to his whole self. His love wasn't based solely on physical attraction, although that was a fundamental part of their relationship. He also admired her: he loved her voice, her mannerisms, her style, her sense of humour – even the way she walked. But he also cared about Antonia and her well-being, and he wanted to believe that she loved him just as much.

He thought about the Ffryes Mills matter. He knew how important helping Ettie was to Antonia and he wanted to help her find evidence that proved Ettie's ownership. He had already told Antonia about the conversation he'd overheard between Aaron Jaygo and Ethan, but he didn't want to seem to be trying to lead the enquiries. He didn't want Antonia to feel he was taking over her project or just trying to impress. But there was something he could do that might help her without any apparent interference: he would try to find out more about the mysterious Ethan and how he planned to secure the ownership of Ffryes Mills. He had an idea that might allow him to get an insight into their plans. He would contact Florence Prideaux and ask for her help. Whatever he found out, he would pass on to Antonia. There was a danger that Florence might be working with Aaron, but he trusted his sense that she was honest and told himself that she would be unaware of Aaron's skulduggery. Peter searched the Ministry of Tourism's website, found Florence's contact details and emailed her.

> *Hi Florence, this is Peter Devon, Antonia's friend. You remember we met on Happy Days? I wonder if you could spare some time for a chat. I'd like to ask a small favour – something that we should keep between ourselves for the time being. Could we meet for a drink after work? I could do tomorrow, Tuesday, at six, if that suits you? Please let me know. Many thanks, Peter.*

Florence's reply came back in a couple of hours.

> *I would be happy to meet, Peter – sounds intriguing! Can I suggest the Spinnaker restaurant at the far end of the marina boardwalk? But can we make it 6.30? You will need to book a table. Florence*

Peter instantly confirmed and said he would make the booking. He did so, then with another thought he phoned the Sheer Rocks restaurant to make a booking for Saturday evening for Antonia and himself. The ambiance, the wonderful food and drinks, and the sunset and views out to sea would create the perfect romantic atmosphere where they could relax and focus on their future together, not on work or their break-up. It was their favourite place and he wanted to show Antonia how strongly he felt about her. He would message her to ask if she would like to have dinner.

***

After work, Peter had time to go home, shower and change for his meeting with Florence. He parked, then took the short walk to the Spinnaker. It was the first time he had been there. It had a great view of the marina and the far side of the harbour. Dusk was just turning to night. After a cloudless afternoon, the sky was coming alive with stars and the warm, jasmine-scented breeze ruffled the waves in the harbour.

Florence was right about needing a reservation – the bar and restaurant was nearly full. The buzz of conversation created an appealing atmosphere and staff moved swiftly between tables with carefully balanced trays of glasses and plates. He decided he would like to bring Antonia here at some time in the future.

Florence arrived right on 6.30 p.m. Peter was stunned when she walked towards him. She had also clearly been home after work – he couldn't believe she would have worn the outfit she had on now to the office. Her pink and lime-green shirt-dress was fitted at the waist and low-cut, flattering her full cleavage. She'd left the last few buttons open to show her long, slim legs. She wore high white sandals that emphasised her height and elegance. She wore subtle eyeshadow and her smile was emphasised by deep pink lipstick. He hoped she had not got the wrong idea about their meeting; he had not invited her on a date.

"Hi, Peter, lovely to see you." They kissed each other on the cheek. "Hope I'm not late."

"No, not at all. Great to see you, too. Thanks for coming." Peter pulled Florence's chair back for her, catching a wave of her deeply scented perfume as he did.

"My pleasure."

"What would you like to drink?"

"Just a small glass of white wine, please. I have to pace myself. I'm going on from here to meet my boyfriend at Sugar Hills. It's his birthday, but that's not until 7.30. I hope an hour will be enough?"

Peter let out a small breath of relief. He had jumped to the wrong conclusion! He immediately relaxed and thought about why he had asked to see her. "Of course – that's perfectly fine."

The waitress took their order and Florence congratulated Peter on his new job. She said that Antonia had told everyone in the office the news. They discussed where he would live in St John's and the best local restaurants.

"I guess I should mention what I wanted to talk about," said Peter. Florence nodded.

"It's in connection with the Ffryes Mills land. Do you know it? It's just behind Ffryes beach."

"I do. And I know the story of Ettie Foster and her claim to own the land."

"Yes, exactly. Well, I can tell you that it is highly likely to be true, but at the moment there are some issues in proving it. I'm sharing this with you in strict confidence; Antonia and I discovered some papers that may well help to confirm that Henrietta Foster is the rightful owner."

Florence looked amazed. "Antonia has mentioned the Ffryes papers to me but I didn't know they are connected to Ettie."

"Oh good, We want to do the right thing for Ettie, if we can. I should tell you that I haven't told Antonia I've arranged to meet you. She has enough on her plate at the moment at work, so I didn't want to burden her."

"I see, but how can I help?" said Florence.

"The reason for keeping all this confidential is that there are other parties who are trying to claim ownership of the land because they want to develop it, probably for a hotel or resort, and one of them is Aaron Jaygo."

Florence's eyes widened. "No! He's not into property development. For sure, he's very keen to see Antigua become renowned for the best-quality resorts, but I can't see Aaron being involved in actually building and operating a hotel or anything like that."

"I agree, but he is working with someone who will develop the land – an American by the name of Ethan. I don't have his surname, but I'd like to know more about him: the name of his company, for example, and any other connections he has on the island. I was hoping you might know him. Recently, I was at Diana's bar and Aaron and Ethan were there. I couldn't help overhearing their discussions about their plans for Ffryes Mills."

"Well, I don't know him personally, but I'm aware that Aaron has had meetings at the ministry with a man called Ethan Krasky. I have seen him a couple of times and noticed his American accent. When he signs in the visitor's book, he gives his company as LWP – I think it stands for Lee-Wind Properties," said Florence.

"That's helpful to know. Thank you so much. I will see if I can discover what their plans are with Ffryes Mills."

After chatting about where Florence was going later that evening, Peter glanced at his watch. "It's nearly 7.30, you will have to be away soon. Before you go though, can I just ask again that, for now, you keep all this confidential? I will let Antonia know what my enquiries turn up once I have something solid to tell her."

"I understand and I wish you luck. It would be wonderful if Ettie's ownership could be settled once and for all. Will you let me know what progress you make?"

"Yes, of course, and if you have anything else to tell me, just call me," said Peter.

Florence looked out at the road, past Peter's shoulder. "I can see my taxi waiting."

They stood to leave. Peter held Florence's arm, they kissed on both cheeks and walked out of the restaurant together. Peter didn't take any notice of the group of people walking in from the sailing club, heading for the Spinnaker, chatting and laughing. At the front of the group, looking over at the restaurant, was Antonia.

THIRTY-FOUR

Antonia glanced at the bedroom clock. It was nearly 2 a.m. and she still couldn't get to sleep. The image of Peter seeming to be affectionate with Florence tormented her and drove all other thoughts from her mind. They had looked natural together. Antonia recalled that they had got on well when they met on *Happy Days*. Florence was a beautiful woman and Antonia agonised that Peter was attracted to her. She had worried about that before. The dress she had been wearing was designed to show her figure to its best advantage and Peter was wearing a dark-blue shirt she hadn't seen before – very flattering. Did she really know him as well as she thought she did? Would he allow himself to be tempted by a beautiful girl?

What could be the reason for their meeting, other than the start of a romance? Why had they met like that, in the open, in a busy restaurant? She knew that Florence had a boyfriend. And Peter, why would he brazenly meet Florence when he had just declared his love for her so strongly?

But she knew that the emotions that physically attract people could fog good sense and create desires that overwhelm reason. Antonia also recognised that the devils of the night could conjure up negative feelings in her mind and create traumas that defied logical thinking. And jealousy was a powerful emotion, driving anger, suspicion and distrust. She was determined not to succumb to a negative state of mind and got up and went to the kitchen for a glass of water. She stood and looked out at the marina. The Spinnaker was well out of sight at the far end of the boardwalk, but all she could see in her mind was an image of Peter and Florence together.

She smiled an ironic smile at how she had so readily accepted Peter back; the good news about his job had certainly lifted her feelings for him and her hopes for them to have a lasting relationship. But she couldn't help asking herself if she had been a fool to take up where they had left off, without giving herself time to think about what she really wanted and whether he really did have the enduring feelings for her that he talked about. And could she still regard Florence as a good friend? What was the expression? 'All's fair in love and war.' If Florence had feelings for Peter, then she wouldn't hesitate to ditch her friendship with Antonia. Would she?

After a while, she went and sat in the living room. The Ffryes papers were on the desk and she decided she would take the afternoon off the next day and go to the museum in St John's again. They might have a record of the fire – and within those records, hidden away, could be a mention of the sale to Nathaniel Foster. The plan settled her mind. She was ready to go back to bed and she fell asleep instantly.

***

Minutes after waking, Antonia felt depression hit her. The images of the evening before were just as vivid in her mind and she was now convinced that there was something going on between Florence and Peter. Her mood was as low as it could get. She physically felt the weight of her disappointment: she was lethargic, short of breath and had no appetite for breakfast. It was going to be difficult in the office, facing Florence, but Antonia had no intention of confronting her and making a scene. She would be polite and professional and keep her mind on her job. She only had to stick it out for the morning.

When Aaron arrived in the office, Antonia felt angry that he was involved in a plan that would see an old woman deprived of her property and placed in a home against her will. But she had to keep her opinion to herself for the time being – and keep an eye out for a visitor by the name of Ethan.

The morning passed quickly and she decided to have lunch in her flat before driving up to the museum. Parking was always difficult in the streets around the port, but she managed to find a spot near the cathedral, just minutes from the museum. She was pleased to see the welcoming smile of Janelle on the front desk and asked her if Sharon Dubois was available to assist her again with her research. Janelle showed Antonia through to the reading room and within five minutes Sharon arrived.

"Good to see you again, Antonia," said Sharon. "How can I help you today?"

"Hi, Sharon. It's the same subject – the ownership of Ffryes Mills. You may remember you kindly looked up the Land Registry records for information on ownership of the property since the 1890s and there was nothing on record. What I am focusing on now is a fire at one of the other plantations owned by the same person. It probably happened the year before I believe the Ffryes estate was sold to Nathaniel Foster, so that would be 1891. Apparently, Nathaniel saved the son of the plantation owner from the fire and, as a reward, the owner sold him Ffryes Mills for just one pound. There might be some mention of the sale in among the records of the fire."

"That's quite a story, but we really need to know the name of the plantation where the fire occurred. Do you have this?" asked Sharon.

"No, I'm afraid not, but the name of the person who we believe sold Ffryes Mills to Nathaniel was Arthur Arkwright, of Somerset, England, and Antigua. If we can find details of other plantations he owned and look up records of a fire, then that's where there's a chance the sale to Nathaniel might be mentioned."

"Right, let's have a look." Sharon turned towards the large screen and keyboard on her desk and spent a few minutes scrolling through the historical documents and journals section of the archives. She found a list of plantation owners in 1890. "There's nothing listed for Arthur Arkwright, but there was a plantation called Cove Point where the apparent owner was someone called Henry Arkwright. That could be his son. You know, the profitability of plantations and estates was very often shared among family members for tax reasons. There were all sorts of taxes and excise duties to be paid and, not surprisingly, plantation owners did all they could to avoid them. But when it came to selling the estate, it would be the true owner who entered into the sale agreement."

"What sort of documents exist in the archives for Cove Point?" Antonia asked.

Sharon scrolled through the images of the papers in the archive. "I can see the usual accounting ledgers and there are plantation output figures: sugar, rum and molasses; expenses incurred, such as costs for timber and food for employees; details of the ships the products were exported on. Hang on, this is interesting." She pushed the screen round to show Antonia. "Look… in the annual accounts for the year ended 31st December 1890, it notes the rebuilding costs for the boiling house following a fire. Total costs incurred were £1,245, which would have been a fortune in those days. But then it shows on the income side: £1,095 received from Lloyd's underwriters – they were obviously insured for fire damage, although it didn't cover the whole cost."

"That's brilliant, Sharon – it confirms Ettie's story. All we have to prove now is that it resulted in Mr Arkwright deciding to sell Ffryes Mills to Nathaniel."

"There's one more point of interest here, look. Under the schedule of costs for the year, it individually lists the wages for overseers and managers. There he is, Nathaniel Foster, age twenty-one, overseer. So we know he was an employee at the time. The only thing missing is a record that notes the sale of Ffryes and that should, of course, be held in England."

"Yes, but as I said, the solicitors don't have any record of the sale. Nevertheless, this has been really helpful. Thanks so much for making time to look through the records with me."

"That's what we're here for. Pleased to help where we can. Do come back in if you need any further assistance."

"Thank you, Sharon, I will."

***

Thrilled with the information she had obtained from the museum, Antonia arrived back at her car in a positive frame of mind. She took her phone out from her handbag to check her messages: there were a couple from work and one from Peter. She opened Peter's straight away and read it with a mixture of delight and confusion.

> *Hello darling, just planning ahead for this weekend. I hope you're free on Saturday evening. I have booked Sheer Rocks for seven. I can pick you up from your flat at 6.45. Hope this is OK. xx*

Antonia realised she had completely forgotten about Peter and Florence while she was at the museum, and the relationship between them – whatever it was. Peter's text jolted her worries back into her mind and she sat in the driver's seat to give herself time to think. She had to decide whether to challenge him or just carry on as best as possible and hope that any romance between Peter and Florence would fade away. She wanted to take his invitation to dinner and a romantic evening at a wonderful location at face value. It was the Peter she knew and loved; she couldn't face the idea that he might be the type of person who would cheat on her.

On the drive back to Jolly Harbour, she made a decision. She would accept the invitation to dinner – it would give them a chance to talk. What more could she do to give Peter a chance to be open and honest? If he couldn't be open and honest with her, they had no future together.

THIRTY-FIVE

Antonia started the weekend with a 7 a.m. gym session, then showered and collected together the Ffryes Mills papers and her notebook and placed them in her tote bag. As she walked to her car, she revelled in the perfect weather: it was warm without being fiercely hot and there was a welcome breeze off the sea, with only a few puffy clouds high in the sky.

It was only 9 a.m. as she started the drive down to Ffryes. Once there, she parked under the thatched sunshades behind the beach and took the steps up to Diana's bar for breakfast. There were several other people doing the same, including the well-dressed expat couple she had seen many times before. This time the man smiled and waved at her, and she remembered he worked on *Happy Days*. Antonia smiled back and walked over to their table. She felt she should make an effort to get to know them; she had few friends on the island and she wanted to be sociable.

"Good morning. Lovely day, isn't it?" said Antonia.

"Beautiful," said the lady. "Won't you come and join us? My name is Lisa and this is my husband, Mike."

They all shook hands and Mike pulled an extra chair over from an adjoining table.

"I'm Antonia Casey-Brown. I live up at Jolly Harbour, but I love to come to Diana's for the view and the lovely food."

"We're the same," said Lisa, smiling and waving a hand towards the sea. "Gorgeous, isn't it?"

Diana came to the table to take their order. They chose a fruit platter to share, a basket of pastries and coffee all round. Antonia said, "Diana, is Ettie here this morning? I'd like a quick chat later, if possible."

"No, she doesn't work on Saturday mornings; she's probably at home. You know where that is, of course."

"Yes, thank you."

"You work at the Ministry of Tourism, don't you?" Mike asked. "You were on the day cruise we put on for them."

"Yes, I'm the tourism planning manager. My job is to bring new ideas to Antigua's tourism offering and make sure there is something for all visitors, all around the year."

"Sounds fun. What are you working on at the moment?"

"Various projects. My particular interests lie in cultural tourism, the history of the country, and the story of slavery and emancipation – but not everyone at the ministry agrees with me that this type of thing will attract visitors."

Mike leant forward. "I'm sure there are lots of cruise ship visitors who would enjoy seeing more of the history of the place. They see beaches and duty-free shops on every stop they make in the Caribbean!"

"I agree. In the meantime, though, I'm working on promoting high-end hotels and resorts, and yachting weeks, of course. Perhaps we will add cookery schools and painting and writing retreats."

"Brilliant!" said Lisa.

"Do you live at Tamarind Hills?" asked Antonia, gesturing to the development at the other end of the beach.

"Yes, we've been here nearly four years," said Lisa. "It's a beautiful place to live. There's a mixture of residents and holiday lets. Some villas and apartments are mostly unoccupied or just used once or twice a year by the owners. More of a financial investment than a regular second home."

"Or third or fourth home for the seriously rich," said Mike.

They all laughed. "You work on *Happy Days*, Mike, but what do you do, Lisa?" Antonia asked.

"I work part-time at the Financial Services Commission, in the insurance department. I was with Lloyd's in the UK before coming out here."

Antonia looked puzzled.

"Lloyd's of London – the insurance business. The commission here were interested in my experience and offered me a job in the department dealing with the supervision of insurance firms in Antigua and Barbuda. You know, making sure they play fairly with their customers. It suits me to work just two days a week and keep my hand in. I'm not sure how long I will keep it up, though. I want to enjoy the sun, sea and relaxation. We didn't come out here for me to spend all my time in an office!"

"Yes, it is beautiful, isn't it? Did you know that there's a risk that the land down there behind Ffryes beach might be developed in the future? It would really change the outlook from Tamarind Hills," said Antonia.

"Yes, there have been attempts in the past, but since it seems to be impossible to verify who owns the land, we feel quite safe that nothing will be built there," said Mike.

"Ah, well, strictly between us, the true owner might soon be able to prove ownership. I'm helping her get her case together to file with the Land Registry office. Don't worry, she has no ambition to develop the site – except maybe for building a small house."

"How interesting," said Lisa. "I assume you mean Ettie, who works here? We have heard her story, but what evidence does she have that will satisfy the Land Registry?"

Antonia instinctively knew she could trust the couple and felt perfectly comfortable telling them about the papers, how she and Peter had discovered them, and the help she had received from the national museum. She described Ettie's family history and how she lived rough in the windmill. She went on to say that she had become aware that an American property developer was also making investigations and trying to prove they owned the site.

After they had finished their breakfast and a second coffee, Antonia said she was going to visit Ettie.

"Look, if there's anything we can do to help, just let us know," said Mike.

"That's kind of you, thank you. I'll keep you in the picture. I'm often here for breakfast."

"And for drinks in the evening – we've seen you with your handsome partner," said Lisa, smiling.

"Yes, true. We love the sunsets here." Antonia stood to leave. "See you soon."

As she walked down the steps to the beach and the path across the scrubland towards the windmill, Antonia smiled at Lisa's choice of words. Peter was very good looking and thinking of him as her partner made her tingle. He was very special to her. She just hoped that his love was the lasting kind.

THIRTY-SIX

Picking her way through the long grass and spreading ground ivy that surrounded the windmill, Antonia found the narrow but well-trodden path leading to the dark, ominous entrance. She shuddered at the thought of Ettie actually living in there. How could she sleep at night? The badly fitting door that she had seen on her first visit was resting just outside the windmill and she saw faint beams of light inside, shining down from the louvred roof panels.

"Hello!" Antonia called. "Hello, Ettie? Are you there? Can I come in?"

There was no answer, but Antonia stepped into the entrance and waited a few seconds for her eyesight to adjust. She noticed the not-unpleasant hazy smell of wood smoke and cinnamon from the small fireplace, where a kettle sat.

"Ettie, it's me, Antonia. We met before, here and at Diana's."

Antonia recalled from her first visit the alcove inside the doorway where Ettie had hidden. She turned round and there she was, sitting on the bench.

"What you wantin' now, girl?"

"Ah, Ettie, there you are. I'd like to have another chat with you, if that's possible? Perhaps we can go over to the beach, sit under a sunshade and have a nice cold drink?"

"What you want to talk about?"

"I have some information on the ownership of Ffryes Mills to share with you."

"You gonna ask lots more questions?"

"Maybe a few, but there will be no pressure. I think you will be interested in the things I have to tell you."

"OK, Miss Antonia, let me get myself ready."

Antonia went and stood outside, glad of the fresh air.

In a few minutes, Ettie emerged, plainly dressed in a white cotton shift dress and a boater-style straw hat with a bouquet of small flowers tucked under the headband. Her feet were bare. They walked the short distance to the beach, which was busy with weekend families, and found one of the last available sunshades. After settling Ettie in, Antonia went up to Diana's and brought back a couple of glasses of mango and orange juice.

Opening her tote bag, Antonia said, "I have here some old papers that tell of the sale of the Ffryes Mills plantation back in 1892 to someone called Nathaniel Foster. Is that your great-grandfather, do you think?"

"Yes, ma'am. It's what I tell everyone. He was the owner of the plantation."

"And he came to own it following a fire…," Although she had heard it before, Antonia wanted Ettie to relate the history in her own words.

"Like I say before, Great-grandfather was a young man working at a plantation. It was up in the hills somewhere and there was a fire in the sugar boiling house. He saved the owner's boy and was given Ffryes as a reward. Only a small plantation, but make him a landowner and sugar grower. Make him a big man with money. I'm the last descendant of Great-grandfather, but without those papers showing the ownership, everyone call me Mad Ettie."

"Well, we may be able to prove them all wrong. Look at these papers," said Antonia. "Peter and I found them in the sea, in an old box. As well as having these records of the sale, I have spoken to the Antigua museum, which has papers noting the fire – it was at a plantation called Cove Point and Nathaniel was an overseer there at the time of the fire. Pretty strong evidence that the plantation could have been sold to him."

Ettie smoothed out the papers and looked in smiling amazement at the map and drawings. "This is my windmill!" she said, tapping the sketch of the plantation. "All this land around is mine."

"That's what we need to prove."

"How you goin' do that?"

"Well, we must take these papers to the Land Registry office in St John's. They will look at any other proof of title to the property that might be in existence and any other claims of ownership. If there are none and they are happy that these papers are genuine, then they will register the property in your name and you will be free to do what you like with it. Perhaps you could sell it for a lot of money!"

"I don't want to sell, girl. I want to build a small house for me for when I get old, that's all, with no one objectin' like they have done in the past."

Antonia smiled to herself. Ettie was probably approaching seventy already. "That's a great idea."

Antonia walked Ettie back to the windmill and wrote out her address and phone number on one of her Ministry of Tourism business cards. She left it with Ettie on the little table.

"Promise me you will get in touch if any problems arise," said Antonia. "And if it's OK with you, I will go and visit the Land Registry office and let you know what they say. This could take a couple of weeks."

"That's fine with me, girl, thank you."

***

That evening, back at her flat, Antonia reflected on what the day had brought her. She was so pleased Peter had got in touch. She had a feeling that he had booked Sheer Rocks as a romantic gesture, an effort to rebuild their relationship, and she couldn't deny that she was burning to see him again, even if doubts over his association with Florence plagued her thoughts. She wouldn't do anything rash that would result in them splitting up again. A small voice in the back of her mind reminded her how delighted she had been on hearing about Peter's new job and that he was staying on the island. She had been pleased that they could resume their relationship – perhaps they would even marry and have children. *No, no! This is far too early to be thinking about such things. Don't get carried away. Take things steady*, she said to herself. *Give him time and space to decide if he wants the same things.*

Antonia felt trepidation at the task ahead of her in proving Ettie's ownership of Ffryes Mills. Peter's story about Aaron and the American meant she needed to get the required proof in front of the Land Registry people before anyone else could make their case. She resolved to make an appointment as soon as possible.

THIRTY-SEVEN

E ven from her desk at the far side of the office, Florence couldn't help overhearing Aaron Jaygo's phone conversation with Ethan Krasky. She heard them set up a meeting – Ethan would be coming into the office at 3 p.m. She knew that Antonia would be out on a visit to English Harbour and several other staff would be working from home or off on visits to the port authority and hotels. The ministry's offices would be quiet and Aaron never shut the door to his office. She made sure she had a notepad and a pencil handy.

At around 3.15 p.m., Krasky arrived. He walked straight through and sat down in Aaron's office. He opened the slim leather document case he carried and took out a bundle of papers.

"The courier arrived yesterday and brought copies of the deeds and other documents. They show the sale in 1880 to Arthur Arkwright. What we now need, of course, is the onward sale papers from the Arkwright family trustees to Caribe Landco in 1970. These are being sourced by my associates in the US and will take another week to arrive. We will then show that we took over Caribe Landco in 2018, so the

Ffryes Mills estate is therefore ours. Once this is confirmed by the Land Registry, we can get going on the hotel development."

"These associates in the US – how exactly will they find proof of the sale in 1970?"

"Don't you worry about how and where, Aaron. All you need to do is make sure your cousin at the Land Registry is convinced that the documents are genuine and date from the 1970s. I will let you know when the whole caboodle is submitted and you can lean on your cousin, OK?"

"Ethan, as I have said before, I don't want to be associated with anything illegal and, you can be sure, nor does Elijah."

"Hey, relax. All I'm saying is that the papers for the sale to Caribe Landco have been lost for many years and we have only just discovered them in our offices in the US. Our lawyers will attest that they are genuine. There's nothing wrong with that and you can be satisfied that the development will bring more prosperity to the island. You always say that high-class tourism is the key to the prosperity of all Antiguans and you are the leading light in this work."

Florence knew that this sort of flattery would be effective with Aaron; he was always looking for praise for his highbrow ideas. Krasky understood how to manipulate him. Florence had no doubt that the documents evidencing a sale in 1970 would be forged; Krasky had implied as much. It was clear that Krasky had involved Aaron so he could use his cousin who worked at the Land Registry. Florence did a quick internet search and found an 'Elijah Trent' at the Land Registry, who chaired the committee that reviewed ownership appeals. That must be him. Florence had heard all she needed to know. She made some notes, then pointedly concentrated on her own work as Krasky left the office. She would ring Peter in the evening and update him on what she had heard.

***

Peter was clearing his desk and briefing the staff who would take over his role on the status of his projects. He had been leaving work early in the last few days before moving up to St John's and treating himself to a run or swim before going home. This evening, it was a quick front crawl the length of Ffryes beach and back. After showering at the house, he prepared his evening meal, a pan-fried salmon fillet with linguine in a tomato and herb sauce. As he was clearing up the kitchen, his phone, sitting on the coffee table in the living room, rang. His heart jumped. He hoped it was Antonia. He recognised the number, sat down on the settee and put his feet up, intrigued by what Florence might tell him.

"Hi, Florence, good to hear from you. How are you?"

"I'm well, thanks. Are you OK?"

"Sure, all good. Have you some news for me?"

"I have indeed. There was a meeting today in the office between Aaron and Ethan Krasky. Look, don't think badly of me, but I did some listening in of my own."

Peter laughed. "No problem. It's all for a good cause! And it's not difficult; Krasky is so loud."

"That's true. They discussed the ownership of Ffryes Mills. They have received details of a sale to someone called Arkwright in 1880. But the interesting bit is that Krasky is having papers prepared in the US detailing a sale in 1970 to a company called Caribe Landco, which is now a subsidiary of Krasky's organisation, Lee-Wind Properties. That's how he will claim to be the rightful owner of Ffryes Mills. He will say the sale papers were recently found in their US offices, but I'm certain those papers will be forgeries."

"That's incredible Florence, but won't they have to convince the Land Registry people that all their documents are genuine in order to get ownership confirmed?"

"They will, but they have a secret weapon – the chair of the land ownership review committee at the Land Registry is Aaron's cousin. Aaron's job is to make sure his cousin approves the application. Krasky is putting pressure on Aaron by emphasising the benefits to Antiguans that the new development will bring, which he knows is so important to Aaron."

"And, of course, there's the $10,000 fee Aaron is being paid…" said Peter.

"Really? I didn't know about that."

"Yes, Ethan mentioned it when I heard them talking at Diana's bar. It's a bribe, of course, dressed up as a consultancy fee."

"Then he's being a real rat, depriving Ettie of her right to the land and making ten grand in the process. Not such a hero after all." There was venom in her words.

"No, indeed. I'm going to have to tell Antonia about the plan to submit forged papers to the registry people. I'm seeing her tomorrow evening. The documents she has prove the plantation was sold by Arthur Arkwright to Nathaniel Foster in 1892, so it's impossible that a sale was made in 1970 by the Arkwright trustees to Caribe Landco. I'm so glad you rang. You have helped so much."

"I would like to say it has been a pleasure, but it's upsetting to see Aaron, who is essentially a good man, get involved in this business."

"Yes, but isn't he just being a fool? He's clearly being pressured by Ethan Krasky. I'm disturbed by the bribe he is taking, which undermines any good intentions he has," said Peter.

THIRTY-EIGHT

With five minutes until Peter was due to arrive, Antonia checked herself again in the mirror in the hallway. She was delighted with her new dress: she loved having all the designer shops in Heritage Quay, which sold a vast range of women's clothes. Tourists from the cruise ships were always keen to buy stunning outfits for their gala dinner and dance evenings. Her black dress had silver-grey silk trimmings on the arms and neckline that echoed the way her pearl necklace glistened. Antonia felt that black always showed off her suntan to best effect. She left her hair down and natural. Her black patent leather shoes had a four-inch heel – daring for her.

But Antonia frowned as she looked in the mirror. A knot in her stomach wouldn't let her relax as the image of Peter with Florence played on her mind. The day before she had decided that she would ask him outright if he was involved with her, but now she dreaded having the discussion. She might get an answer that she didn't want to hear. If he admitted there was something between them, then what could she do other than walk out of the restaurant – and out of Peter's life? She knew there would be no going back this time; she couldn't tolerate a relationship where she had no trust in her partner.

A knock at the door snapped her out of her gloom and sent a thrill of excitement through her.

"Come in, I'm nearly ready."

"Wow, you look fabulous tonight, darling." Peter kissed her on the lips.

"Now look what you've done. I'll have to redo my lipstick!" Antonia flashed him a smile as she went into her bedroom. After a couple of minutes, she returned, carrying a wrap and her handbag. "Shall we go?"

***

They sat on high stools at the outside bar of Sheer Rocks for a pre-dinner drink. "I think I'll have the featured cocktail, a pineapple planter's punch," said Antonia.

"I'll go for a Manhattan."

The maître d' brought them menus and said their table was ready for them whenever they wished to go through.

"This is such a beautiful place. I think I can see lights over on Montserrat," said Antonia.

"Yes, the air is really clear tonight. Look, there's a cruise liner in the distance – no doubt coming into St John's. Good for your line of business!"

"Yes, the tourism season has gone well this year."

"Any joy with developing Antiguan history tours?" Peter asked.

"No, it doesn't really excite the hotel owners and tour operators, but Betty's Hope is always popular with visitors and the museum down at English Harbour."

"That's a shame, but you're working on other plans, aren't you?"

"Yes, there will be more events next year – some sailing regattas, new cookery tours and classes. There's a lot of interest in Antiguan and Caribbean cuisine in the UK now that we have the celebrity TV chef, Andi Oliver. She's a great ambassador for Antigua and I'm hoping to book her as the host for some of our events."

"Sounds excellent."

"Yes, she's quite a character and she can tie in visiting her family on the island with our programme of cookery courses. They're going to be hosted by Sugar Hills."

"Great idea, Antonia."

"Thanks. I thought you might have heard about this already…" Antonia couldn't help letting her thoughts about the relationship between Peter and Florence spill over. She just prevented herself from adding, "Surely Florence told you".

Peter looked puzzled. "No, it's news to me. Great news at that."

Antonia recovered her composure. "Ah, yes, of course, announcements about next year's programme have not been made public yet."

Peter caught the eye of the maître d' and signalled that they were ready to go through to their table. Antonia was delighted with the position they had been given at the far end of the decking. They had an unbroken view of the night sky and the cove below the cliffs, where waves broke in luminescent foam on the rocks. Pink and cream lanterns hung above them and a single candle glowed on the table.

After they had placed their order, Peter leant across the table and took Antonia's hand. "I'm so glad we're together again, Antonia. You know how much I love you. I just don't know how we came to fall out over my job. I'm sorry I acted the way I did."

"And you know I love you, too. We both took a position over our work. I'm really glad you were offered the new role." Antonia squeezed Peter's hand and smiled. "I'm sure you will do a great job. They're lucky to have you."

"Oh, I say. You're so kind, my lady," said Peter in his best upper-class accent.

The starters arrived. They had both ordered oysters with a tamarind and lime dressing, accompanied by a glass of chilled Muscadet. Antonia's main was the baked snapper and Peter chose the grilled beef rib.

After the beautiful meal, Antonia was basking in the glow of love she felt for Peter – something she had never experienced before. But was it real? Would it be something they would share for life? She sat back, looked out to sea and took a slow, deep breath. She knew the time had come. "There's something I'd like to ask you, Peter. Something that needs an honest answer."

Peter looked concerned. "What is it, my dear?"

"I saw you at the Spinnaker with Florence on Tuesday. I was just back from a sailing trip with people from the club. You looked so happy together. Florence is so glamorous… and I wondered if you and she were… well… close and—"

"Whoa, stop there! Absolutely not!" Peter gasped. "How can you think that I would even flirt with someone else, let alone become close? We met to talk about Ffryes Mills. I was planning on telling you what we, well, she had discovered. I wanted to help you find evidence that would confirm Ettie's ownership, but without burdening you with extra work. My idea was to do some research and let you know the results."

"Right…" Antonia said cautiously. A fleeting shiver of regret shot through her as she realised she would look like a jealous, controlling girlfriend who wouldn't let their partner speak to another girl. She couldn't deny that she had been fretting over it. She needed to know if there was anything going on between them, but would her questioning damage their relationship and drive a wedge between them? She felt she had to continue, even if it meant risking Peter being irritated at her probing. "But how did that involve Florence?"

"I asked her to see what she could find out about the American I saw Aaron having a drink with at Diana's. And what she told me was incredible. After dinner here, I thought we'd go back to your flat for coffee and I would update you. But I can tell you now instead. Florence found out that this American, his name is Ethan Krasky, is fixing the evidence so that his property development company will get ownership of the land and build a hotel on the site. Florence is very much on your side in trying to prove Ettie's case. Of course I'm not in a relationship with Florence. It's you I love, one hundred per cent."

Antonia totally relaxed; the knots of anxiety inside her had gone. She laughed gently as tears of happiness welled in her eyes. "Only one hundred per cent?" she asked.

Peter said, "Sure, she's attractive, but she has a boyfriend…" He hesitated, suddenly aware that he was digging himself into a hole, then stuttered, "And anyway, I'm not interested in anyone but you."

***

After dinner, Peter asked the waiter to book a taxi back to Jolly Harbour. He would collect his car in the morning. In the ten-minute ride, he managed to summarise, without using names, the conversation that Florence had overheard.

As soon as they arrived at her flat, Antonia put the coffee machine on and took out two glasses. "I bought a special bottle of rum this week – would you like to try it?"

Peter picked up the bottle and read the label. "Appleton Estate 21 year old Jamaican rum. Very nice."

"I thought you might like it. A special treat to round off dinner."

Peter wrapped his arms around Antonia and they kissed softly and repeatedly, with both of them lingering to enjoy the moment. He whispered, "How beautiful you look tonight, my darling."

"So you said and you're not so bad yourself. Come, let's take these through to the living room. You can put some music on, if you like."

Peter chose a Latin compilation with samba, rumba and salsa songs. "What will you do about Ffryes Mills?" he asked.

"Well, tomorrow is Sunday, so there's not much that I can do, but next week I will speak to the solicitors in Wells and tell them what we've discovered and get their guidance on what to do next. In the meantime, I'm happy to forget about Ffryes Mills for a few days, to be honest. I have other things to think about." Antonia turned the music down low and poured two more small measures of the rum. "Come here," she said.

They sat on the two-seater and slowly wrapped themselves together. Antonia kicked her shoes off, curled her legs under her and rested her head against Peter's shoulder. The firmness and warmth of his body set her heart racing. He brushed his hand through her long hair and down her back, then ran his fingers along her thigh. Without either of them consciously leading, they stood and walked through to her bedroom. Peter pushed the door almost closed, and in the soft light they slowly undressed each other and enjoyed their togetherness for the rest of the night.

THIRTY-NINE

The shrill ringing of her mobile phone startled Antonia awake. She wrapped herself in her silk dressing gown and dashed into the living room to take the call, puzzled. Who could be ringing so early on a Sunday morning? As she grabbed the phone, she saw a number she didn't recognise.

"Hello, Antonia Casey-Brown speaking."

"Oh, hello, Antonia. It's Diana here. I hope I'm not disturbing you?"

"Hi, Diana, that's perfectly OK. How can I help?"

"It's Ettie. I'm afraid she seems to have disappeared and I was wondering if you could shed any light on where she might be. She didn't show up for work last night, so I went over to the windmill first thing. She wasn't there and I have searched the area without any luck. I found your card in the windmill with your number on it, hence my call."

"Goodness, this is worrying. I'll come over straight away and help you search. Does she have any friends that she might be staying with?"

"No one that I know of and, of course, she has no family left."

"Why don't I stop at Bolans on my way down? There's a fruit stall there; I can ask if anyone has seen her."

"Yes, good idea. The morning staff will soon be arriving and I will ask them if she has said anything about going away."

"Right. I'll see you in less than an hour."

Peter walked through from the bedroom in his boxer shorts. "Problem?"

"Yes, a bit of a mystery. It seems that Ettie has gone missing. That was Diana on the phone. She said Ettie didn't arrive for work last night and she isn't in her windmill. I'm going over there to help look for her and I'll stop at Bolans on my way. I'll have a quick shower first."

"Look, while you're having your shower, I'll make some coffee. If you can delay five minutes, I can have a shower and come with you. I'll drive, if you like?"

"Would you mind? It would be great if you could come. And there are some croissants in the kitchen you could warm up."

"No probs. Now, go and have that shower!"

***

Peter parked under the sunshades at the back of the beach and they walked over to Diana's.

"So good of you to come, Antonia. Hi, Peter. Did you have any luck at Bolans?" said Diana.

"No. The woman selling fruit knows Ettie, but said she hadn't seen her."

"Right. I really have no idea where she could have gone. She seemed perfectly fine on her Friday evening shift."

"Have you called the police?" said Peter.

"No, it's too soon to do that. They won't respond to a missing person for a day or two."

"Why don't Peter and I go over to the windmill? We might find something that would give us a clue."

"Well, sure. I did have a good look around, but you never know."

Antonia and Peter stopped off at the car to collect their sunhats. Although it was only mid-morning, it was over 30 degrees with high humidity. There was a faint breeze and enormous rain clouds were forming out at sea. Antonia knew to expect a heavy downpour by lunchtime.

As they approached the windmill, Antonia took Peter's arm and pointed to the long grass. "There are tyre tracks going right up to the door. That's new. There's been a car here!"

"You're right – look, the tracks continue up the lane."

"Let's go into the windmill and have a look round."

Antonia swept aside the dried leaves where Ettie slept. On a small table were a plate, some odd pieces of cutlery and a half-full glass of water. She picked up Ettie's straw hat and a shawl from the floor. In the alcove were a pair of old sandals. There was nothing that would suggest why Ettie had disappeared – nothing was really out of place.

When the pair emerged into the open, the rain clouds were almost overhead and the wind had got up. The air was humid and silent lightning flashes filled the clouds out to sea. The horizon had vanished; the rain was a continuous lead-grey wall and it was heading inland.

"We'd better get going if we're to beat the rain before we get back to the car." Peter started to head off towards Ffryes beach, but Antonia went a few yards the other way, following the tyre tracks.

"No, Peter, come this way. I have an idea."

"Are you nuts? We'll get absolutely soaked!"

"That doesn't matter, the rain is warm. Come on!"

Peter ran to catch up and slipped his arm around Antonia's waist. "Well, Miss Marple, what grand ideas do you have?"

"Don't make fun of me; this is serious," Antonia said. "I have a feeling that Ettie might have made for the hills if someone came to her windmill who she didn't like. This is the path the guide took us on when I did the trek up Mount Obama. There are old goatherds' huts higher up – she might be hiding in one of those."

The pair found the going tough as the steepness of the hill increased. The dense undergrowth and exposed tree roots had them stumbling and tripping as the rain pelted down. They stopped and looked into a couple of derelict huts, calling out Ettie's name, but without any sign of her. When they came to an outcrop of huge rocks, Antonia sat down on the largest boulder, wiped the rainwater from her face and looked back towards Ffryes beach to gauge how far they had come.

"Bloody hell, this is hard work," said Peter. "Do you really think the old lady would manage to get up here?"

"Possibly. She's been living in this area all her life. Climbing a hill is no hardship. Come on, let's go a little further."

As they started off again, Peter slipped down onto a knee and yelped. As he stood up again, a rivulet of rain pouring down the hill washed over his feet. He grabbed a tree trunk to steady himself.

"OK, we can go on a bit more. You see that ledge up there, about a hundred feet up? Let's make that our target. If there's still no sign of her, we go back. Agreed?"

"Agreed," Antonia said reluctantly.

The last section of climbing was slippery and physically demanding. As soon as they reached the ledge, gasping, Antonia called Ettie's name again and again, then waited. After a while, feeling depressed that they hadn't found her, Antonia suggested that they turn round and start to work their way back. Going down proved to be more difficult and dangerous than ascending, as the wind battered them and the rain was relentless. Finally, they reached the rocks where they had rested on the way up and sat down again for a few moments.

"You were right, I must be nuts bringing us up here!" said Antonia. "It's not so steep from here on, though. Go on, lead the way."

Cautiously, Antonia stood up and began to follow Peter, but then she heard a voice call out from behind the rocks to her left.

"What you two wantin'?"

Antonia whirled round to face the sound.

FORTY

Antonia and Peter walked Ettie back down the hill, along the path that took them to Diana's. They arrived half an hour after the rainstorm had passed. Now, the sun shone in a gin-clear sky. They almost dried out in the heat and took a table at the back of the decking, away from other guests. Diana sat down with them.

"She was halfway up Mount Obama, hiding from some men who came to her windmill yesterday afternoon. Apparently, Ettie had been out collecting some wild papayas and pineapples when she saw them arrive," said Antonia.

Diana took Ettie's hands in hers and gave her a light-hearted scolding for running off and not seeking help from her. A waitress came over and Diana asked for a basket of bread and pastries, a plate of hors d'oeuvres they could share, bottles of water and a large French press of coffee.

"Tell us again what happened when the men came, Ettie," said Antonia.

"They come in a big white car, like a Jeep, but it have black windows. Two men, smart-lookin' but not nice-lookin'. I saw them go in my windmill and when I went to shoo them away, they try to grab me, but I ran up to the rocks and a cave I know. It's dry up there, and men in nice clothes don't like to climb the hill. Stayed all night, but then I saw you comin'." She looked at Antonia and Peter. "Hope you don't give me up to those men."

"Oh, Ettie, don't think such a thing!" said Antonia. "We want you to be safe. Maybe you should spend some time with a friend for a few days. Do you have anyone you could ask?"

"No. I don't want to leave the windmill. People say if you leave, you give up your rights."

Diana leant forward. "Well, at least stay here tonight. You can shower and there are some clean clothes in the staffroom. You can sleep in my office, if you don't mind the settee?"

"You a good girl, Diana. That's what I do tonight, thank you, child."

"Great. Why don't you go through now and have a shower and get changed?"

As Ettie walked away, Peter turned to Diana. "Any idea who these people could be?"

"None, I don't know anyone with a white four-by-four with blacked-out windows."

"What were they doing?" said Antonia. "Surely they wouldn't kidnap Ettie to get her off the property, would they?"

Peter answered, "They might if they believed it would help their case in getting ownership."

Antonia clasped her hands together. "Tomorrow, I'm going to call my contact at the Antigua museum to tell her who is claiming ownership of the estate and how they're proving it. No, in fact, I think I will take the morning off and go into St John's and meet her. She's really helpful and I'm sure she will help me work through the Land Registry website and see what claims for ownership have been filed."

"Would you like me to come with you?" asked Peter.

"Thanks, but there's no need, not at this stage. It might be helpful if you could speak to Florence – tell her what I'm doing and ask her to give us any further information she can get. Mention the visit the two men made to Ettie yesterday and the car. She might know something about it."

"Will do. Now, let's get back to your flat. I'm sure you'd like a change of clothes."

***

Antonia had a quick session in the gym on Monday morning before she gathered together all her papers on Ffryes. She checked the museum website. Opening hours were from 9 a.m., which gave her time to drive up to St John's, find somewhere to park and pick up a cup of coffee. She arrived just before nine and was pleased to see Janelle already at the reception desk.

"Good morning, I wonder if Sharon Dubois is here this morning and can give me a little time?"

"Good morning. Welcome back to the museum. Sharon's not at her desk at the moment, but she will be here shortly. Let me take you through."

Antonia was given a seat next to Sharon's desk and took a few moments to think through what exactly she was hoping to achieve. She reflected that it was great they had the sale papers dated 1892, but if these were insufficient evidence of ownership, what exactly would satisfy the Land Registry people? And if Aaron and the American had filed their claim, what documents did they have that disproved Ettie's claim?

Sharon came hurriedly over to her desk, apologising for her lateness, even though it was only ten past nine.

"That's quite alright, Sharon. It should be me apologising – I've come without an appointment on a Monday morning," said Antonia.

Sharon placed her coffee flask and cup on her desk. Antonia declined her offer of a cup for herself. Sharon switched her computer on. "Now, how can I help?"

"I hope I'm not taking advantage of your kindness in assisting me, but I believe you may be able to find the answers to a couple of questions I have."

"On the subject of Ffryes Mills?"

"Yes, that's right. There have been developments – not entirely happy ones."

Sharon poured her coffee and sat back. "Intriguing. Tell me more."

"An American property investor, who I won't name at this stage, in collaboration with a well-known Antiguan, is about to file documents with the Land Registry that will try to verify that the estate was sold in 1970. The sale is supposed to be from the trustees of the Arthur Arkwright estate to a company called Caribe Landco. This firm was taken over by the American's company, called LWP, at some point since 1970, so he will claim to have rightful ownership and can apply to build on the land. The thing is, we have evidence that Arkwright sold the property to Nathaniel Foster in 1892, so Arkwright's trustees couldn't possibly have sold to Caribe Landco in 1970. We believe that the documents being filed are forged."

"Goodness me, that's quite a story," said Sharon. "But why haven't you gone to the Land Registry with this information?"

"I haven't yet because I'm unsure if the 1892 papers that we have will themselves be believed or seen as fakes. I want to have some form of independent evidence that substantiates the sale, some form of official record. I've mentioned the fire at Cove Point to you before, but unless we can find something new, it doesn't help us prove that Ffryes Mills was sold to Nathaniel Foster. At the same time, I want to check that there is no evidence that would verify the 1970 sale. There can't be, of course, unless it has been forged." Antonia held back on mentioning that Aaron would be putting pressure on his cousin to approve the application from LWP, as that could be seen as slanderous or, at least, malicious gossip.

"Right. Since we have already searched for information on the fire, what I suggest we do now is search for evidence of a sale in 1970, or thereabouts, in the museum's archives, as well as the publicly available information on the Land Registry website. It will take some time, but if we don't find anything, it would reassure you that no such sale occurred. How does that sound?"

"That would be brilliant, Sharon."

"Do you have anything else to do in St John's this morning? You could come back around 11.30 to see what we have found, if that would suit you?"

Antonia sensed that Sharon wanted the time and space to do the searches. Although she had nothing in particular to do, she decided to take the hint and go for a walk, tour the shops and perhaps have another coffee somewhere. "Sure, that would be fine," she said. "See you in a couple of hours. Before I go, can I say, you are taking a lot of time and trouble on this project of mine. Is this really all part of your job?"

"In the broadest sense, yes. We don't just keep old relics and curiosities here at the museum; I see our role as influencing the present and the future by what we can learn from the past. If you, or we, I should say, are able to unquestionably verify Henrietta Foster's ownership of the estate, that's a positive for the work of the museum."

"I see. Thanks again, Sharon. You're very kind."

***

When Antonia walked out of the museum, she was hit by the heat from the sun, which was already stifling. She decided to walk through Heritage Quay to find the Frigatebird restaurant, tucked away in Radcliffe Quay, one of the oldest parts of the harbour. The tall palm trees wafted steadily in the breeze and gave welcome shade over the array of tables and chairs on the terrace outside the restaurant. She ordered orange juice, coffee and – as a special treat – a banana and honey flapjack.

Tourists from two cruise ships were wandering around the shops, deciding between splashing out on another handmade silver bangle or a new Sea Island Cotton shirt. With time to kill, Antonia was enjoying people-watching. After the waitress had brought her order, Antonia noticed a couple approaching the restaurant and she realised it was Lisa and Mike, her friends from Diana's.

"Hi, Antonia! Great to see you. I didn't know you liked to come here," said Lisa.

"Hi, Lisa. Hi, Mike. It's my first time here, I have to kill some time before a meeting. What about you? Are you regulars?"

"Guilty as charged. Notoriously regular, I'm afraid, the maple syrup pancakes here are excellent," said Mike.

"Maybe for you!" said Lisa as she turned to Antonia. "What's he like? I will have my usual healthy option, the tropical fruit cocktail."

"Good choice," said Antonia. "Why don't you join me?"

"Splendid!" said Mike.

As they ate, the three talked about the cruise ships that had arrived in the early hours, whose passengers were now spreading out across the island and spending their very welcome US dollars. Antonia glanced at her watch. It wasn't quite 11 a.m.

"Is your appointment a work thing here in St John's?" asked Mike.

"No, it's at the museum. I'm still looking into the Ffryes ownership question that I mentioned to you. They are doing some research for me and it should be done in about half an hour."

Lisa asked, "How are you getting on with settling the ownership rights to the land?"

"We're almost there. We have the 1892 papers for the sale to Nathaniel Foster and we know about the fire where Nathaniel rescued the owner's son. We know they're genuine, as we found them sealed in the tin we managed to pull out of the sea. Problem is, we need absolute proof that the estate was sold to Nathaniel as a result of the fire. The archives staff are going through their records right now."

"Have you not discovered anything about the fire in the records?"

"The only definite reference is in the accounts for the estate where the fire occurred, called Cove Point. The records show it was owned by a Henry Arkwright, although it was probably really owned by his father, Arthur. The accounts mention the cost of rebuilding and the payment by the insurers. And they say that Nathaniel Foster was employed as an overseer on the plantation at that time."

"Do you know who the insurers were?" said Lisa.

"Yes, the accounts say it was Lloyd's underwriters."

Lisa and Mike looked at each other; both were wide-eyed and smiling. "Well, that's very interesting," said Mike. "You may remember we mentioned that Lisa worked at Lloyd's in London before we came out here."

"Yes, I remember."

"I'm not surprised the plantation was insured at Lloyd's – it's famous for the policies its underwriters have provided worldwide for the past three hundred years," said Lisa.

"Incredible really how business could have been transacted at such a distance." Antonia looked at her watch. She was in danger of being late back to the museum. She took out a business card, swapped phone numbers with Lisa, then stood up to leave.

"Best of luck and keep us informed, won't you?" said Mike.

FORTY-ONE

Florence was suddenly aware that she had heard the name 'Ethan' float out of Aaron's office. He was on the phone. She sat up, tuned into his voice and picked up her notepad and pencil. This time, there was a lot going on in the office and she could only hear Aaron sporadically – and of course only his side of the call.

"What do you mean, 'escaped'? Are you saying you tried to kidnap her?" Aaron's irritation made him virtually shout. "Safe place or not, you can't just take someone from their home and lock them up somewhere!"

Florence's phone rang. She couldn't ignore it, so she took the call. It was Peter, contacting her as he had promised Antonia he would. Florence explained quickly and quietly that she was tied up and would call him back as soon as possible.

"I've no idea where she could be. She has no family." Aaron seemed to have calmed down and was now speaking more authoritatively. "Look, if, as you say, the papers are being filed on Thursday, it will take about a week for the case to be reviewed. I will speak to my cousin, emphasise how important the development is for Antigua and make sure he doesn't raise any unnecessary objections."

A visitor arrived at the front desk for an appointment with the marketing team. Florence showed her through to the meeting room, then returned to her desk.

"OK, Ethan, if you insist, but personally I don't think she has to be moved away from the land for it to be declared abandoned and unoccupied." The general background noise in the office now blocked out most of what Florence could hear. "… No, the Land Registry people will just regard her as a squatter and leave it to the new owners to remove her… Alright then, understood, so long as the place she is kept is warm and secure and she is well fed… OK, tomorrow it is."

Florence picked up her handbag and phone and went to leave the building for a few minutes so she could call Peter back. But as she walked to the door, Aaron called over to her, asking her to come into his office. She suddenly felt a twinge of fear. Had Aaron realised she was listening to his call? She quickly recovered when he said he wanted to discuss the copy for new posts on the ministry's website. Florence tried hard to contain her irritation as Aaron slowly went through the draft text. It took almost an hour and when that was done, he asked her to look through some CVs that had come in for some new positions they had advertised. Florence's frustration built. The moment the clock reached noon, she told her colleagues she was going for an early lunch.

She looked at Peter's number on her recent calls list and wondered if he would be at his desk or in a meeting. She dialled anyway and the phone rang five times before he answered.

"Peter, it's Florence. Sorry I couldn't speak to you earlier. Are you free to talk at the moment?"

"That's quite alright. Now is perfect, the office is empty. I called you to update you on something and ask if you had heard anything more."

"Yes, I have some news, but you go first," said Florence.

"OK, first I should say that on Saturday afternoon, a couple of men arrived at Ettie's windmill and tried to take her away. She managed to run off and then spent the night up on Mount Obama. Diana alerted Antonia and me, and we found her yesterday morning. She spent last night at Diana's."

"Well, that explains something. Aaron had a call this morning with Ethan. Although I couldn't hear everything, I gathered that some people had been to the windmill looking for Ettie. I think they are going to try again tomorrow."

"Right, then we must ensure that she keeps away or, at least, that someone stays with her. Ettie mentioned that there were two men and they came in a white four-by-four with blacked-out windows."

"OK. There's also something else I heard. The papers proving ownership are going to be filed with the Land Registry on Thursday and it will take a week for them to review. Aaron is going to put pressure on his cousin to wave the application through."

"I'll let Antonia know. She will want to file her papers, too, but she's also hoping to get more information about the fire at Cove Point to back up Ettie's claim. She went to the museum this morning and I'm seeing her tonight after work for a drink at the Mango Tree, so I'll have an update. It's really vital that we have information that corroborates the sale to Nathaniel Foster in 1892 – without it Ethan could submit a more convincing claim."

"Antonia will be in the office this afternoon. It will be impossible to talk there, but perhaps I can join you both for a drink after work?"

"Yes, sure, brilliant idea. We can then plan what to do next. I'll see you at about 5.30. In the meantime, I will give Diana a call and ask if she can keep Ettie there for a few more days."

***

Peter arrived slightly early at the Mango Tree, so he ordered a beer. The expats at the bar had already started their evening of drinking and tried to persuade him into joining them. He declined as politely as he could and found a table in a quiet corner. He didn't have to wait long before Antonia and Florence arrived.

Antonia went through her meeting at the museum and Florence related the call she had partly overheard. The news of Ethan filing their claim with the Land Registry in just three days' time energised Antonia. "We have to go ahead with the submission using the papers we have. Surely the forged documents that note the sale in 1970 will be seen for what they are and the application will be thrown out when the registry people see that it can't be true because the Arkwrights didn't own the property at that time?"

"Yes, it makes sense to file Ettie's claim as soon as possible," said Peter. "I spoke to Diana and she will try to make sure Ettie stays at the restaurant for the next few days. We really should get her approval for the submission – it's her property after all. Any mistakes we make could result in her claim being ruled out, once and for all. She wouldn't thank us for that."

"No, you're right, we are taking on a hell of a responsibility in filing the claim," said Antonia.

Florence said, "Don't think about that. You're doing the right thing for Ettie. Without your papers, she would have absolutely no chance of claiming her inheritance."

Antonia clapped her hands together. "Well, let's give it a go. I'll drive down to Diana's this evening and tell Ettie what we're doing, so that she can agree or disagree with the claim. I will get everything ready tomorrow and file the papers on Wednesday."

"Let me do the driving. I can take you there, then we'll have dinner," said Peter, taking Antonia's hand. He was more than pleased to be actively supporting her.

"Would you? That would be great. Thank you, darling."

FORTY-TWO

Diana's bar was relatively quiet, not surprising for a Monday evening. Fortunately Ettie was able to be released from her work in the kitchen for half an hour to sit with Antonia and Peter. At their request, Diana joined them. After talking through what they were planning to do, Ettie was happy for them to go ahead. Antonia asked for Diana's opinion, since she was in effect the closest thing to family that Ettie had. Diana recognised that if Antonia's papers were not believed to be genuine and if Ethan's claim was convincing, then the estate might be lost forever. But it was a risk that had to be taken.

When Ettie and Diana returned to work, Antonia and Peter ordered their dinner: spicy lamb cutlets with rice and fried okra. They both drank mango and orange juice.

"Why don't we take a walk along the beach? You've been so busy at work, and with all your efforts on the Ffryes affair you need some downtime," said Peter.

Antonia was delighted with the idea. A bright half-moon and the sparkling starlight lit up the waves as they lapped rhythmically along the sand. They pulled off their shoes and walked in the shallows, their arms around each other's waists.

"It's so nice to be here on the beach where we met," said Antonia. "You frightened me when you first spoke to me!"

"I was only pointing out Montserrat; didn't mean to sneak up on you."

"You asked me to have a drink up at Diana's. I wanted to, but I didn't want to seem like an easy pick-up. A girl has standards, you know."

"I didn't expect to see you again, so I had to invite you then and there!"

They walked to the far end of the bay, just before the first of the Tamarind Hills villas. Antonia suggested they sat at one of the round picnic tables that were permanently fixed along the top of the beach.

"They're beautiful houses, aren't they?" said Antonia.

"Yes and expensive, but wouldn't it be wonderful for us to live there? Swimming every day, great views of the sunsets, handy for Diana's and Sheer Rocks."

"Getting a bit forward, aren't you, Mr Devon, thinking we might live together?" Antonia laughed and squeezed Peter's hands.

Peter seemed to miss the humour in Antonia's voice. He gazed out to sea with a serious look on his face. Antonia's comment had taken the wind out of his sails. Slowly, he turned to face her. "Yes, I suppose I am, since we don't actually know all that much about each other or what brought us here to Antigua, our families. You have never spoken much about your past life or previous relationships."

"I could say the same for you. But does that matter? What's important is for us to believe in each other, to love each other and to be honest with each other. I don't want to linger over the past; it's the future I think about. And yes, since you ask, it would be wonderful to live with you in a beautiful place like this."

Peter took a long, slow breath. "Tell me about your last partner. What happened? I don't want to make the same mistake."

"Oh, you fool, you're nothing like Steve! I have never loved anyone the way I love you. He wasn't a bad person, but we were more like good friends than partners. The problem was: we wouldn't admit it to each other. He found someone else and for a long time he stayed with me, but at the same time he was falling in love with this other woman. It was only after I found out about her and challenged him that he decided to go off with her. Sure, I was hurt for a long time, but I rebuilt my life and found the courage to come and live and work on the island. And then I met you. Maybe you should tell me about your girlfriend and how you came to be here? Don't say it was for the job; the real reasons are always deeper than that."

"It's not a lot different to your story, but it was me who was in the wrong. Her name was Stephanie. She was a professional singer and dancer. She was a very headstrong and determined person, supremely self-confident and ambitious. In fact, my move to Australia that I told you about was actually to follow her. She had secured a leading role in a production at the Sydney Opera House. She was destined for the big time."

"Wow, that's incredible. She must be quite the star," said Antonia.

"Life for her was all parties and late nights, and my life was the dull routine of working in a water recovery plant. I foolishly got involved with my secretary – I know, it's a cliché. The silly thing was I didn't love my secretary, it was just a bit of amusement, I suppose. Filling the boring evenings when Stephanie was working. I learned a lot about myself in that episode of my life, how stupid and thoughtless I had been. Anyway, Stephanie found out and gave me my marching orders. It was exactly the excuse she needed to dump me and concentrate on her working life in the theatrical world. And she's now married to a Broadway producer and lives in a multi-million-dollar apartment in

New York. I hope she's happy, because I certainly am, sitting here with you."

"Me too. I'm glad we've had this chat. I want us to be open with each other and to have no secrets."

"I want that, too, my love," said Peter. "And so, I felt I needed to get away from Australia, so I applied for the job here. It's been the right decision. I love the island, not to mention a certain young lady…"

"Young-ish, you mean."

They laughed and Peter pulled Antonia closer.

"Hey, look, coming along the boardwalk, it's Lisa and Mike," said Antonia. "They must be heading for Diana's. Shall we join them?"

"No, let's get back to the car. I think I'd rather spend some time alone with you, if you know what I mean, back at your apartment."

"Yes, I think I do…"

They kissed briefly, wrapped their arms together and disappeared into the darkness behind the beach.

FORTY-THREE

First thing the next morning, after Peter had left, Antonia spent an hour writing a letter to the Land Registry detailing Henrietta Foster's claim to the ownership of Ffryes Mills estate. She named Ettie's father and grandfather and made references to the family records held by the Civil Registry office. She was happy that everything was in order. The papers from the tin were smoothed out and bound in a document folder. Antonia reflected that the papers had been in the sea for over one hundred and thirty years: they were a little faded, but otherwise still in perfect condition. Whoever had sealed the tin never knew how important it would be generations later.

Antonia called Florence to say she had to call into the Land Registry. Would she mind telling a white lie if Aaron should enquire as to her whereabouts and say she was on a visit to the port in St John's? Florence agreed immediately and wished her luck. Antonia then phoned the Land Registry office and made an appointment for 2 p.m.

The next task Antonia had to attend to was to drive down to Diana's; she needed to get Ettie's signature on the letter and check all the documents. Ettie could read and write, but the old-fashioned handwriting on the deed of sale and the letters from the 1890s was beyond her. Antonia explained everything and went through the claim letter slowly and patiently. After Ettie had signed the letter, Antonia breathed a sigh of relief. At last she could go to the Land Registry armed with all the evidence that was required. And they were filing the claim ahead of Ethan Krasky's company, which Antonia hoped would work to their advantage by setting the minds of the registration people in favour of Ettie's claim.

***

The Land Registry offices were modern, bright and clean. The staff in the open-plan office looked quietly industrious as Antonia was led through to the meeting room by the receptionist. A pot of coffee and three cups were laid out. Antonia was advised that Mr Jameson and Mr Trent wouldn't be long. She was a touch annoyed with herself for feeling tense and apprehensive. Why the hell should she be worried? It was just another meeting in another office; she did this all the time for work. Within five minutes the two men had arrived. They shook hands and introduced themselves as Elijah Trent, director of registration, and Andrew Jameson, senior analyst.

"Welcome to the Land Registry office, Miss Casey-Brown. How can we help you today?" Trent asked, while Jameson poured the coffee. He was the only one with a notepad and pen in front of him.

"I'm here to submit a claim for ownership of a piece of land in the Ffryes area known as Ffryes Mills. I am representing Miss Henrietta Foster, who is the rightful owner of the property." Antonia wanted to start off by giving a clear message.

Trent sat back, a look of surprise on his face, but said nothing. Jameson responded. "We have had claims on this land in the past. We know about Mad Ett— I mean, Miss Foster and her claim, but she has never been able to substantiate it."

"Yes, but now we have original documents that detail the sale of the estate in 1892 from one Arthur Arkwright to Miss Foster's great-grandfather, Nathaniel Foster. You will notice that the sale price was just one pound. This was because Nathaniel rescued Mr Arkwright's son from a fire at another plantation called Cove Point and the sale was a way to thank Nathaniel. Henrietta's line of inheritance has been verified by the Civil Registry. The whole story is laid out in this letter from her, the sale documents and some letters included with the deeds. I think you will find they are all in order and they prove that Henrietta Foster is the owner of Ffryes Mills."

Antonia's heart rate was increasing, but she kept telling herself to remember to breathe and relax. Trent gave her a menacing stare that she felt was designed to indicate his disbelief in the story.

Jameson took the file and leafed through the contents. "This is very intriguing, Miss Casey-Brown, but where did these documents come from?"

"They were in a sealed deed box that I found in the sea at Ffryes beach a few months ago. You will see they refer to a law firm, Carter, Kingsnorth, in the city of Wells in Somerset, England. I have been in touch with the firm that took over Carter, Kingsnorth's affairs – they're called Cathedral Law. They are unable to confirm the sale in 1892. The only records they have date back to the purchase by Arkwright in 1880. I have been in touch with your colleagues here and I understand you have no record of the 1892 sale either. All this explains why the ownership has never been confirmed in previous claims. There was just no evidence." Antonia paused, took a slow breath and delivered the key element of Ettie's claim. "But gentlemen, there is now. These papers."

Elijah Trent suddenly came to life and sat forward, his hands open and raised. "The challenge will be to prove the documents are genuine.

There have been many attempts in the past to claim ownership of properties, particularly old plantations, across the island. You will need better proof than these documents. Of course, even if you succeed, the estate may have been sold on again by Miss Foster's grandfather or father."

Antonia was getting annoyed at Trent's negativity. "Well, that's unlikely, as Ettie's father often related how the family owned the land. He would have known if his father had sold it on."

"It is most unfortunate that the law firm in England has no records of the sale. And the reference to the fire at Cove Point is irrelevant to this matter. I'm sorry, Miss Casey-Brown, but I cannot see how the claim can be shown to be valid." Trent sat back and folded his arms, looking satisfied that he had discounted Antonia's case.

But Andrew Jameson was more positive than Trent. He spoke up, risking a glance over at his boss. "What we can do is ask one of the archivists at the Museum of Antigua and Barbuda to take a look at the documents you have found and give a view on their likely origins. Their opinions are not conclusive, but we can take them into account when we consider Miss Foster's claim."

Antonia was delighted with the suggestion, as she felt the museum people would be supportive of Ettie's claim. "Thank you, that makes sense. Shall I leave these papers with you now?"

"Yes, please," said Jameson. "It will take several days for the review to be carried out. I will be in touch as soon as we have an answer."

"Thank you so much."

Antonia was shown out of the office, feeling more positive about the claim than ever before. However, she would not have been so optimistic if she had known what Trent was planning.

FORTY-FOUR

L ate that afternoon, in the Ministry of Tourism, two men sat each
side of a desk and looked at the phone. This time, the office door
was shut. "You said he would ring at 5 p.m. It's now nearly half past. I'm
not waiting much longer. Who does your cousin think he is, keeping
me hanging around like this? What the hell does he want anyway?"

"I've no idea, but please be patient, Ethan. It's not easy for Elijah.
He has to keep my involvement confidential, otherwise he could be
taken off the case. No land ownership registration can be considered
where there's a personal connection. He probably wants to give us some
advice on the application."

"We can't pussyfoot around here, Aaron. The application is going
in tomorrow, whatever your cousin says."

"Understood, but you want to give it the best chance of success,
don't you?"

"Amen to that," said Krasky, just as the phone rang. Aaron pressed
the conference call button. "Good evening, Aaron Jaygo speaking."

"It's Elijah, Aaron."

"Right. I have Ethan Krasky here in the room and you're on speaker."

"Good evening, Mr Krasky."

"Yeah and good evening to you, pal. Now, can you tell me what it is you have to say?"

Aaron cringed at Krasky's arrogance.

"Well, there's something you should know in regard to the application for ownership of Ffryes Mills, which I understand you will be submitting this week."

"Yeah? Well, give it to me."

"Another application was filed today. A certain party acting for Miss Henrietta Foster has discovered papers that could prove she has legal ownership. We will have specialist archivists give their opinion as to whether they are genuine or not. If there is any doubt, then the claim will be rejected."

"You can prove these papers are fake, right?"

"Possibly, but there is also the question of the provenance of your submission and the one from this other party. As I understand it, you have a strong case in that you have had a US firm of lawyers attest to the discovery in New York of the 1970 sale papers. The other claim has no supporting papers, so their case is looking weaker at the moment."

"That's good to hear, Elijah. Tell me, who is filing on behalf of Ettie Foster?" asked Aaron.

"I can't disclose that. It's not on public record, but it doesn't matter who delivered the claim to the office; everything is in Miss Foster's name and signed by her."

"Well, listen up, Elijah, you better make sure the document geeks give you the right answer, you understand me?" said Ethan. "A little gentle persuasion might help. Sow a seed of doubt – you are the top guy, after all."

"I cannot influence their decision, Mr Krasky! It's outrageous to suggest such a thing."

"OK, OK, take it easy. You want the hotel development to go ahead at Ffryes, don't you? Makes for good tourism, good for employment, good for Antigua's dollar earnings."

"Well… yes, that's true."

"OK, so it's easy. Reject the other claim and approve my company's by next week, then we all go home happy, right?"

"I will see what can be done, but I'm not promising anything. Good evening gentlemen." Aaron ended the call.

Ethan Krasky banged a fist on the desk. "Let's make sure there are no slip-ups here, Aaron. Who do you think might be filing on behalf of the old lady?"

"The only person I can think of is Diana. You know her, she runs the restaurant next to Ffryes beach and kind of looks after Ettie."

"Maybe we should send some of our team down there to have a little discussion with her."

"Oh, great! And what good would that do, Ethan? For a start, your boys screwed up with trying to take Ettie to this secret home. I wouldn't trust them not to do something stupid. And don't think Diana is alone – she is well liked locally."

"Alright, what the hell. Our application is irrefutable, so no matter what the Land Registry document analysts say, our papers will do the job. Along with a little encouragement from you to your cousin, Aaron. There's a lot of dough riding on this deal and I'm relying on you."

Aaron didn't like Krasky's tone of voice nor the look on his face. He questioned how long he would put up with this foreigner.

FORTY-FIVE

On Saturday morning, the group of friends sat around the table at the end of the veranda at Diana's bar and restaurant. Antonia and Peter had parked moments before Florence pulled up in her car and walked in with them. Diana and Ettie were already at the table. The sun was streaming directly along Ffryes beach and the aquamarine water washed gently over the near-white sand. But none of them were taking in the beautiful views. Ettie had insisted on returning to her windmill and had slept there, untroubled, for three nights, but had risen early to make the meeting this morning. She sat still and alert, ready to hear the update that Antonia had promised she would have. Diana patted her shoulder to give her comfort and reassurance.

In fact, Antonia had little real news. She described the meeting at the Land Registry and the filing of the claim for ownership. She kept the story low-key, not wishing to infer that they had any real chance of success, given the strength of the claim from Lee-Wind Properties. It was this part of the process that puzzled Ettie and she asked for it to be explained.

"The papers that we filed show the sale in 1892 from Arkwright to your great-grandfather, Nathaniel Foster. As well as the deeds, there is the letter that mentions the sale for just one pound because of Mr Arkwright's gratitude to Nathaniel for saving the life of his son in the fire at Cove Point plantation. The problem is: we have no way of verifying the sale or that it followed the fire. The Land Registry might say the whole thing is a fake."

"Them bad people, why they not say the land is mine?" said Ettie.

Florence lifted her hand to speak. Antonia was grateful that someone else was willing to help explain the situation to Ettie. Florence had, of course, heard most of the details from the meetings and phone calls in the Ministry of Tourism offices. "The claim from the American, Ethan Krasky, has all the right papers. They have said they have evidence from the law firm in England that the property was sold to Arkwright in 1880. We have no problem with that. Then, according to Krasky, it was sold by the Arkwright family estate in 1970 to a company called Caribe Landco. They say they have found the original sale papers in their offices. This has been confirmed by a US law firm. Caribe is now part of Krasky's company, Lee-Wind, so that's how they came to own the land. He claims, anyway."

Florence paused before continuing, "But that's impossible, of course, because Antonia has evidence that the Arkwright family no longer owned the estate in 1970; it was sold to Nathaniel in 1892. Their so-called evidence must be fake. The Land Registry will have to decide which story they believe, if they cannot prove that the papers from either party are genuine. Our story lacks impact because we can't prove the reason for the sale."

"Why, exactly, is it so important that we find independent proof of the sale to Nathaniel?" asked Diana. "Surely the deeds and letters you found are sufficient?"

Antonia came back in. "Not necessarily. The people at the Land Registry said they have seen a lot of fake papers in ownership applications over the years, so they are naturally wary. They have to decide if our papers are fake and Krasky's are genuine. The only way we can be sure of proving Ettie's ownership is to send them some form of evidence that confirms the sale. I've spoken to the solicitors in the UK and I've met with the archivists at the Antigua museum and the registry people – nothing can be found."

"Right, I see." Diana looked down at her hands and frowned.

"We just have to wait to hear the outcome this week. We should know by Wednesday. If we are rejected, then we can lodge an appeal, but that is only likely to delay the inevitable. The land will be confirmed as belonging to Lee-Wind and Ettie will be evicted from the windmill."

"That's what I been thinkin'," said Ettie, "so I'm going back to my windmill and not comin' out. I'm not afraid o' them boys in the white car. They can't have my plantation while I'm livin' there."

Diana took her hand. "No, please stay here with me. You know it's safer here."

Antonia tried not to sound overly anxious, but almost called out when she said, "No, just a minute, she may have a point. By staying on the land, she might have rights of occupation, even if it is deemed that she doesn't actually own it." Antonia felt Peter's hand on her arm, but ignored it. She instinctively knew he was about to disagree with her. "That would give us time to challenge the decision, if it goes against us."

"No, I can't agree to exposing Ettie to any danger. There's a real risk that she will be taken away," said Diana forcefully.

Florence nodded in agreement and Antonia accepted that she couldn't argue any further. After all, Diana was Ettie's carer and Antonia was a relatively new arrival on the island. But she also felt how unjust it would be for Ettie if she was deprived of her inheritance by an unscrupulous American businessman. She was all the more determined to ensure that she did everything possible to prove that the Lee-Wind claim was false.

FORTY-SIX

Peter had offered to cook that evening and suggested they call into the Gourmand supermarket to pick up some fresh fish, vegetables and focaccia. He was still organising his flat in St John's after he'd moved in and this would be Antonia's first meal with him there. Although they had been seeing each other for several months now, he still badly wanted to impress her and make her feel special.

The bottle of cava was perfectly chilled and partnered the smoked salmon and cream cheese on toasted focaccia beautifully. Peter had chosen to make one of his favourites: grilled fillets of red snapper with a tomato, olive and cornichon salad. It seemed odd to light candles in the warm Caribbean evening, but they added the intimacy to the room that he was hoping for. Antonia had been working hard at the ministry and on the Ffryes affair and he wanted to help her de-stress. He had a nagging worry that she might blame herself if the decision went against Ettie.

Peter also had something he wanted to say to Antonia. After preparing the salad, he sat down with her and topped up their drinks. "I have something to tell you – a bit of news from England."

"Oh, really?" said Antonia, not always comfortable with hearing news. It could be happy, sad or even dangerous.

"Yep, we are going to have a visitor next month. My sister is coming over for a week. It will be her first visit since I moved here."

Peter thought that Antonia looked uncomfortable at the news. Deep inside him, he knew his sister could be a difficult person to please. She would inevitably judge Antonia and assess whether she was the right person for her brother.

"That's exciting for you. Will she stay here?" said Antonia.

"Yes, I'll have the second bedroom ready by the time she arrives. You two are going to get on really well. She loves swimming and going to the gym, and she's even had some experience in sailing – she had a yacht holiday on the Med a couple of years ago. She also has a pilot's licence."

"Well, you'd better tell me her name!" said Antonia. "You've never said much about her."

"It's Hannah. She lives in London and works at the BBC in the news department. She took an English degree at Magdalene College, Cambridge, then started as a trainee journalist. She's younger than me – twenty-nine."

"Oh, great, Miss High Achiever." Antonia laughed as she spoke. "She sounds very impressive."

"I hope you can take some time off work and we can explore the island with her. I can't wait to introduce you. She'll love you and I hope you will like her."

Peter hoped Antonia was warmed by his enthusiasm and confidence in her. He showed his love for her in different ways; it wasn't always about dining out at Sheer Rocks, walking on a beach at sunset or sex. It mattered to him that she was proud of him, that she wanted to tell the world she was in love with him.

"Yes, I can take time off work," said Antonia. "Shall I make up an itinerary for the week? The main sights: English Harbour, Falmouth,

Shirley Heights, etc. Then some more active things? Maybe a guided hike in the hills, snorkelling on the reef at Galley Bay – that sort of thing."

"Yes, excellent. And I'll book some restaurants – Catherine's Café and Harriett's."

"Great idea," said Antonia. "Now, how's dinner coming on? I'm starving!"

***

After they had eaten, Peter made coffee, opened a decent bottle of rum and put on a CD of Cuban music. They sat close together on the settee: Antonia with her back to Peter; Peter with his arms around her shoulders.

Antonia turned to him. "Have you told Hannah about us? You know, where we are with our relationship?"

"Yes, of course."

"Well, come on, what exactly have you said?" Antonia asked with a laughing lilt to her voice. This was a sensitive question that she had wanted to ask for some time and the news of Hannah's visit gave her the opportunity to ask. She was again asking Peter to be open and honest with her.

"Last time we spoke on the phone, I said we had been together for five months. I told her how we met, what you do."

"Good, good. And anything else?"

Peter laughed. "Since you ask, Miss Casey-Brown, she wanted to know if we were serious about each other."

"And what did you say?"

"I said yes, I believe we are. Certainly I am and I hoped that you felt the same."

Antonia was taken aback. She hadn't dared hope for such an answer. She put her glass down on the coffee table, turned to Peter and wrapped her arms around him. She leant forward and they touched noses. "Well, I'm pleased to say your hopes are fulfilled, because I am certainly serious about you."

"Does that mean we have a future? Are you really thinking we can spend the rest of our lives together?" asked Peter.

"Of course. Weren't you listening? My darling, I love you so much. I can't imagine life without you."

Their admission of their feelings for each other was enough to ignite the passion that simmered in them both. They kissed long and fervently. Peter stood, pulled Antonia to her feet, swept her into his arms and carried her towards the bedroom. Antonia kicked off her shoes and brushed her fingers through Peter's hair. The last things on her mind now were work, the Ffryes estate and Peter's sister.

FORTY-SEVEN

When Antonia's office phone rang a few minutes after 9 a.m. she had a feeling that it would be the Land Registry office. Her pulse pounded as she listened to the secretary to the registration committee introduce herself. Antonia was expecting to hear the outcome of the claim but, annoyingly, she was asked if she could attend a meeting at the registry's offices at some time the next morning, Wednesday. They agreed on 10 a.m. Antonia wondered if she should ask Peter to come along for moral support. Having a second person to listen to the verdict would be useful if it was bad news.

Unfortunately, Peter was unavailable; he had a meeting with the Antiguan government and he couldn't get out of it. Antonia called Diana next and was hugely relieved when she said she could accompany her. They discussed their plan: they'd listen to what the registry people had to say and if it was good news, they would ask when the estate could be confirmed as Ettie's. If it was bad news and the claim was rejected, they would ask why.

***

Elijah Trent chaired the meeting, with Andrew Jameson in attendance and a secretary to take the minutes of the meeting. After the usual pleasantries and coffee, Elijah gave a speech he must have given many times before, outlining the approach the Land Registry took to applications, the problem of forged documents and the need for incontrovertible support for a claim to ownership. He asked if Antonia and Diana had any questions, then didn't wait for a response before opening a thick buff file and pulling out a short, typewritten report. Antonia could see in the file her letter and the papers from the sea, as well as other documents that looked like old deeds and letters. These must be part of Krasky's claim.

Antonia clasped her hands in her lap, she didn't want anyone to see them shaking. She found she could control her breathing, but not her heart rate. Fortunately, Diana seemed quite calm. She had brought a notepad and pen, and sat ready to make notes.

"As you may be aware, we have received two applications for the land known as Ffryes Mills. This is not the first time we have considered claims for this part of the island. Up to now, all the claims were based on false documentation. We are very diligent in our assessment of documents."

Antonia was vexed by Trent's smooth, self-assured way of talking. It felt as if he was lecturing her, but she didn't want to say or do anything that he might regard as disrespectful. The room might have had air conditioning, but it wasn't doing its job. Antonia felt overly warm in the stifling air.

Trent went on. "Both of these applications have their merits and our decision must be made based on the known facts and our opinion of the most credible case. I turn now to the application you have submitted on behalf of Miss Henrietta Foster. We have looked carefully at the papers you claim to have found in a box you took from the sea following Hurricane Lorna last year. The papers are in remarkably good condition, if I may say so, ladies, given their supposed age. Your application – or rather that of Miss Foster – proposes that the estate was sold in 1892 to her great-grandfather, Nathaniel Foster, for the sum of one pound. We find that a staggering suggestion."

Trent looked at Antonia and Diana with a faint smile, raising his eyebrows as if to say, 'You wouldn't disagree, would you?'.

He continued, "Even if the circumstances – the rescue from a fire – are true, we cannot see any precedent for a thank you of this scale. Ffryes was not a large plantation, but giving it away to a twenty-one-year-old overseer seems… implausible."

Antonia's heart sank as she listened to Trent. Ettie's case was withering away. She could see that Trent was enjoying this. She knew that the 1970 sale document from Lee-Wind was a fake, but she couldn't say so, as then she would have to say how she knew this.

Trent turned over the pages of the report and returned it to the file. Sitting back, he drew a breath and placed both hands on the table, palms down, as if ready for any retribution that might come his way. "It is for this reason that we cannot grant ownership rights for the Ffryes Mills estate to Miss Henrietta Foster. Her claim is dismissed. Are there any questions?"

Diana spoke first. "Can we appeal this decision? It seems to me that you have simply decided that Ettie's papers are forged and therefore invalid. In your opinion, you think it's unlikely that the plantation would have been given away as a thank you to Nathaniel, but that's only your opinion!"

"We have two of the best document archivists in the West Indies here in Antigua – they trained and worked in the US before coming here. They could not affirm that your papers from the sea are genuine. You could file an appeal, but do think about it. You have little chance of success. And, of course, the other claimant's documents were supplied by lawyers in the UK and US. That, in itself, would usually satisfy our requirements, but we have also looked at the sale papers from 1970 and we're happy that they are genuine." Trent smiled again.

"The Antigua museum has records that mention the fire at Cove Point – surely that is sufficient to verify the circumstances of the sale to Nathaniel?" asked Antonia.

"Miss Casey-Brown…" Trent took a slow, deep breath. "I'm very aware of the accounting entries for the reconstruction of the damaged building at Cove Point, but that does not constitute evidence of a legal sale of another plantation several miles away."

Antonia knew he was right and she was sounding desperate.

Diana spoke up. "And have you decided on the validity of the other claim?"

Jaygo wriggled in his seat and nervously ran his fingertips over his mouth. "Well, yes, we have. It was a very strong case and the documents provided fulfilled all of our requirements."

"And who is the fortunate claimant?"

"Um… that's confidential at the moment. OK, I can advise you of the name, but please do not disclose this to any party not involved with the Foster claim. Our report will be published by the end of the week and after that all details will be in the public domain. The party with rightful ownership is Lee-Wind Properties."

Antonia had had enough. She felt exhausted and wanted to get out of the office and breathe some fresh air. With a few words of thanks for Trent's time, the pair left the building.

When they got into the street, Diana turned to Antonia and took her hand. "Now, I know you're going to be hugely disappointed, but don't get despondent. I have an idea that will give Ettie a secure future. Let's go back to the Frigatebird for a mint tea and some apple cake. How's that?"

Antonia agreed, although she knew it was Diana's way of offering a small consolation to cheer her up after the defeat they had just experienced.

FORTY-EIGHT

Antonia left a voice message for Peter, telling him about the outcome and asking if he could meet her at Diana's at 6 p.m. They would break the news to Ettie and discuss what to do next – perhaps appeal, but certainly talk about where Ettie should live from now on. She couldn't be allowed to continue as an illegal squatter in the windmill, the men in the white car would soon be back.

Antonia spent the afternoon at work. She wanted to develop her ideas for action and adventure holidays in Antigua. There was a growing interest in guided walking, which would be centred on the mountainous areas of the island, and water sports such as coasteering, kayaking and stand-up paddleboarding. These would need support from specialist operators who would want projected tourist numbers and the marketing plans for the ministry. She was glad to apply her thoughts to work for a while; she had become too tangled up in the Ffryes Mills affair at the expense of her career and, possibly, her relationship with Peter.

However, she couldn't shake off the feeling that there was more she could do on Ffryes. Aaron was out of the office and in a quiet moment

Antonia had a quick chat with Florence to brief her on the meeting at the Land Registry. They focused on what they should do about Aaron: they knew he'd been willing to take a bribe to pressure his cousin into favouring the Lee-Wind application.

"It's just not right, Florence. He shouldn't be allowed to get away with it. I want to have a discussion with him and let him know we know about the bribe."

"But if we call him out on this, he could make our lives at work hell. We may even be forced to resign if we're seen as troublemakers."

"Really? He should be the one to resign – or be fired!"

"It doesn't always work that way in the Caribbean, Antonia." Florence raised her hands, palms out, in mock apology. "He will just say the payment was a legitimate business expense."

"Well, I'm not having it. I'm going to challenge him on the bribe, but without saying how I got to know about it, although he might guess, or he might even know that we worked on this together. I'll try to keep you out of the discussion. I think he will be back in the office tomorrow. We're meeting this evening at Diana's to discuss where Ettie should live from now on."

"No, don't worry, you can mention that I have been involved. I think it might shake Aaron to know that his actions are no secret. Please check with me in the morning before you meet him."

***

The evening air was still and beautifully warm, and the humidity of the day had disappeared. It was perfect for sitting outdoors, illuminated by the stars and candlelight. Peter arrived soon after 6 p.m., straight from work, and Diana had ensured that Ettie was in the restaurant kitchen, ready to join them. Antonia felt her stomach turn over, as she was the one who had to break the news. After a quick catch-up with Peter, Diana joined them, bringing Ettie out from the kitchen.

"Hi, Ettie, it's good to see you," said Antonia, trying to stay upbeat. "Are you well?"

"I'm good, t'ank you." Ettie stared down at her hands in her lap; her fingers were knotted tightly.

"We're here to talk about Ffryes Mills and your claim for ownership…" Antonia felt her breathing falter. She was in danger of becoming so emotional she wouldn't be able to speak. She knew she just had to get on with it. "I'm sorry to say this, but the Land Registry people have refused to accept your claim."

Ettie's eyes filled with tears, but she did not sob. She slowly sat up straight and lifted her chin in a defiant gesture. "My father didn't tell no lies. My land has been stolen from me and soon they will throw me out of my windmill. I will go live in the caves up Mount Obama. No white cars up there."

"No, you don't have to do that, Ettie. I have a surprise for you." Diana had taken Ettie's hands in hers. "We are going to build an extension at the back of the restaurant and you will have an apartment of your own there. A proper bedroom, living room and bathroom. There's no rent to pay; you will be our guest."

"My lovely Diana, you were always a good girl, from the days back on the streets in Bolans, and now you're a proper businesswoman. But no, I will stay with you tonight, if I can, then I will find a place for myself."

"Yes, of course. Stay tonight and we will have a chat in the morning."

***

After driving back to Jolly Harbour, Antonia poured a couple of glasses of white wine and took out a large pizza from the fridge. "How hungry are you?" she said to Peter.

"Very. That pizza looks great, but will it do for two people?"

"I have some salad, cheeses and prosciutto to add, so that would make a nice meal, I think."

"Sounds excellent, thank you. What are you going to do about Ffryes? Is there anything you can actually do?"

"First thing tomorrow, I'm going to see Aaron and have it out with him. No matter how much he dresses it up, he took a $10,000 bribe and I want him to know that we know about it. I discussed it today with Florence and she's worried that we could lose our jobs – or I could, at least. But I don't think he will be so brazen. If we were sacked, there would be questions asked and he'd be risking the bribe becoming public knowledge. No, I'm certain he will want the matter swept under the carpet."

"I think Florence could be right. He might react badly – why take a chance? You know we would come back to that tricky business of our future together if one of us loses our job on the island."

"I've thought of that. If I lose my job at the ministry, I will get something else – at a hotel, perhaps. I've built up some good connections. It won't be as good as my current job, but it would be less stressful and we would be together."

"That's great to hear, but why exactly are you planning on calling him out? What good would it do?"

"I knew you would ask that. It's simple – I don't want him to get away with it scot-free. I want him to squirm and know he has been found out. OK, I admit, there's an element of revenge for what he's done to Ettie. It's too late to reverse the Land Registry's decision and the chances of a successful appeal are almost non-existent, but I want him to feel his guilt."

"I see your point. Alright, but please don't get into a row or resign or anything like that. You know what they say about revenge?"

Antonia looked puzzled.

"Before seeking revenge, first dig two graves."

FORTY-NINE

While having her breakfast, Antonia's phone rang. It was 7 a.m. and the sun had only just risen. Curious as to who it could be, she checked the screen. It was Diana.

"Hi, Diana, what's up?"

"Antonia, it's Ettie. She's out on the headland behind the restaurant, standing on the edge. I think she's going to jump! Can you come down here and help me get her back to safety?"

"I'll be right there. Just keep her talking!"

Antonia quickly dressed and explained to Peter what was going on. He also dressed and grabbed his car keys. Within a few minutes, they were in his car and heading south towards Diana's. The roads were quiet, so the journey only took ten minutes. Antonia and Peter dashed from the car up to the restaurant, but one of the kitchen staff called out to them and directed them to the back of the building, where they almost ran into Diana.

"She's there, standing at the edge of the cliff. She won't come back."

"Let me see what I can do."

"Oh, Antonia, please be careful!"

Ettie was standing a foot from the edge, gazing out to sea, her arms statuesquely pressed to her sides. The cliff face was vertical and foamy waves washed against the rocks more than fifty feet below.

Antonia approached Ettie and spoke softly but clearly, "Hello, Ettie, it's Antonia. I've come to have breakfast with you. Will you come and sit with me?"

"Leave me be, girl. There's nothin' you can do here."

"Come, Ettie, let's sit and have some coffee. That would be nice, wouldn't it? Diana will make us some lovely cornmeal porridge. You like that, don't you? Diana is worried about you out here – let's not upset her. Come with me. Give me your hand." Antonia knew she had to be careful. She wanted to keep Ettie talking and find a way to persuade her to step back from the edge.

Ettie glanced over her shoulder. Antonia could see the streaks of dried tears on her face. "Go away, I say. No business of yours now. You done a good job for my land, but now it's time for me to go, join my family. I want to be with them."

"We can talk about that over breakfast. Please, Ettie, come with me." Antonia stepped forward, trying to keep her balance in the breeze, which was gusting and buffeting as she walked carefully towards the edge to Ettie's side. She felt a wave of vertigo as she looked down at the sea, then pulled herself back. She couldn't help thinking what a beautiful place it was, with a magnificent view along the coast towards Sheer Rocks and Jolly Harbour beyond. Not a place to die, but a place to revel in being alive. She had to focus on Ettie and make her feel the same.

"Ettie, we can go for a walk after breakfast, if you like – we can find some nice shells and pebbles along the beach. Or maybe find some mango trees and maybe papaya – you can show me the best places to go. Will you do that for me?"

"You will find lots of mangoes on Obama. You don't need me to help you."

"But it's much more fun with you. Come, let's walk back down to the restaurant."

Ettie raised her hands to her face and wiped away the new tears that had formed. She was quietly singing a Sunday school song as she looked up into the sky at a pair of swifts that had shot up from the cliff face below. The sun burned down on them. Antonia's mouth was parched and her lips were dry. She coughed and tried again to get Ettie to step back.

"Ettie, you must be tired. Come with me and we can sit and rest together and you can tell me about your sisters. I don't even know their names. It would be lovely if you would tell me about them."

"Elenora and Rosemary – they look after me when I was a kid. They gone now, but I soon join them."

"Such nice names. Come with me and have breakfast and tell me all about— no, no, no!" Antonia screamed as Ettie crossed her arms and stepped nearer the edge. She gazed straight ahead. Her fringe lifted in the breeze and she had a gentle smile on her face.

"Come with me, Ettie, please. Come and join your friends." Antonia shuddered. She felt she might be losing Ettie. She held her arm out and spoke as calmly as she could. "Come, my dear, hold my hand."

Ettie glanced round towards Antonia. Then, without hesitating, she took another step forward. Antonia lunged to grab Ettie, but she was too late. Ettie had stepped off the cliff. Her white dress flapped as she fell. She crashed into the water and Antonia screamed, "No, no, Ettie!"

Ettie soon surfaced and floated in the water, motionless, her arms and legs spread out, face down. The waves pulled her body out to sea and washed it back in again to the foot of the cliffs. Diana appeared next to Antonia, her hand over her mouth and a look of utter shock on her face.

***

Antonia turned to look for Peter, but she only saw his back – he was dashing to the far side of the headland towards Coco beach. He scrambled down between two large rocks balanced on the cliff edge and disappeared from sight. Antonia called his name and ran to the rocks, to see him standing on a narrow ledge about twenty feet below. She called him to come back.

He hesitated, then called out, "Here comes a wave!" As a roller came in, he jumped, as far out as he could.

Peter needed to swim about thirty yards to get to Ettie. When he reached her, he rolled her onto her back and pushed her head up to face the sky, kicking frantically to try to swim over to a small patch of sand at the start of Coco beach. The effort of swimming against the tidal power of the sea and holding Ettie up and out of the water as best he could was draining his energy. He slapped Ettie's face. Her eyes were open, but glazed over. He kept swimming towards the shore. Another large wave crashed over them and he struggled to keep hold of Ettie in the churning water. As Peter pulled her through the sea, she suddenly coughed violently, vomited seawater and gasped for air. Peter was delighted – she was alive! Now that Ettie was regaining consciousness, he knew he had a good chance of saving her, but they were both in danger of drowning if he couldn't get them to the beach. He thought he was making some progress, but, frustratingly, a rip tide was carrying them out across Coco beach bay and, try as he might, he couldn't swim to the shore.

Antonia was horrified by what she was seeing. Peter, the love of her life, looked to be drowning. Ettie might be dead because of her failure. Two people she had come to care about, come to love, were being carried out to sea, soon to lose their lives. All because she had interfered in Ettie's life, stirred up her hopes and expectations, but then failed to secure her property and failed to talk her out of jumping. She was gripped by remorse and guilt.

Diana had the presence of mind to take out her phone and call an ambulance. Then, she grabbed Antonia's arm and shouted, "Come with me! There's a way down to Coco over here!" She pulled Antonia towards a winding path through rough sea grass and over loose rocks, bracken and thorn bushes. Initially, it turned inland, then it headed back down towards the sea. Antonia ran and slid down the path, not thinking about the grazes and scratches she was picking up, trying not to break down into sobs. From the corner of her eye, she saw Peter, way below them, in the clear azure sea, now barely able to tread water, looking totally exhausted, but somehow still holding Ettie.

When Antonia and Diana arrived at the water's edge, they were surprised to see a group of people standing together and looking out at Peter and Ettie. Someone shouted, "Come on, keep going!" Another came to Antonia and said she'd seen a woman, then a man, jump from the cliff. A woman started to wade into the sea, but the others called her back; Peter and Ettie were too far out for her to help them. Suddenly, across the bay, a motor yacht appeared. Spontaneously, everyone started waving and shouting to the yacht, trying to attract the owner's attention. It seemed futile as the yacht continued on its journey south and would soon be around the headland and into Ffryes bay.

One of the men in the group called out, "Hey, that's *Happy Days*! I'll call Captain Thomas." He took out his phone and quickly dialled a number. A few seconds later, the yacht made a hard turn to the left and powered inshore. The man kept talking and the yacht steadily approached Peter and Ettie. When it got near, it killed its engine.

Antonia saw the crew on the yacht pull Peter and Ettie out of the sea and lay them down on the yacht's deck. She felt a surge of hope rise within her and her heart thumped in her chest, then she coughed out a few sobs.

The man with the phone shouted, "Captain Thomas says they're both OK!"

They were safe. Antonia wanted to rejoice and laugh, but she had no energy left. She collapsed to her knees in the sand and cried, in long, deep, body-shaking shudders.

FIFTY

Three days later, Antonia and Diana drove to the Mount St John's Medical Centre to pick up Ettie. They said little on the journey; they had already discussed the arrangements and put them to Ettie for her approval. Diana had made one of her spare rooms at home into a room for Ettie. Ettie had been so full of remorse and apologies at how she had jumped into the sea and also endangered Peter's life that Antonia and Diana were sure she would not do something like that again. Ettie had only suffered bruising and the effects of ingesting seawater, and was now ready to leave the hospital and be taken into Diana's care. Peter had only been retained in hospital for a few hours and, after resting for a couple of days, he was back at work. Ettie was delighted to be staying with Diana's family and as soon as she was fully recovered, she would return to work at the restaurant.

Antonia was still annoyed and frustrated that she had failed to secure Ffryes Mills for Ettie. She reflected that her involvement could have led to Ettie's death; it made her shiver to think about it. But since Ettie was now staying at Diana's and was willing to give up the windmill, Antonia felt some relief at a happy ending of sorts. However, there was one aspect of the matter that she wanted to wrap up; she just couldn't drop it. She was going to face Aaron Jaygo.

***

Soon after 9 a.m. the next day, Antonia walked into Jaygo's office and asked if he had time for a chat. With an outwardly pleasant demeanour, Jaygo agreed, and Antonia turned and closed the door behind her.

"How can I help you this morning, Antonia?"

"I wanted to let you know that I submitted the application to the Land Registry on behalf of Ettie Foster."

Jaygo's faint smile quickly disappeared and he sat back in his chair. "Really? I see."

"I'm pleased to say that Ettie is well. She left hospital yesterday."

"Ah, yes, I heard about the accident—"

Antonia was riled. "It wasn't an accident and you know it, Aaron! She was driven to try to take her own life because she had lost her land. And you also know that was a huge fraud by the American."

Aaron sat up straight and looked indignant. "I know nothing of the sort! The American claim was properly authenticated with all the right documents. I don't know of anything untoward in the matter."

Antonia knew she couldn't prove him wrong, so she moved on to her real point. "But what we both know is that you took a $10,000 bribe for your part in Ethan Krasky's application."

Aaron's reaction was exactly what Antonia had expected. For a moment, she took pleasure in his discomfort. He looked shocked and his eyes widened. "That's not true. That's a ridiculous suggestion!"

"Now, now, Aaron, let's not be silly. You're a poor liar. You were paid $10,000 to influence your cousin, Elijah Trent, to favour the Krasky application. What I want you to do now is admit it. Then, don't you think it would be appropriate if you paid that money to Ettie? I'm sure it would help her in her old age."

Aaron slumped in his chair. "Alright, alright, so I asked Elijah to give Krasky's application the benefit of any doubt, that's all. However, in the end, it wasn't needed, as the registry people were quite happy with the application and had doubts over Ettie's. How did you know that I was involved?"

"Never mind that. It's not just me who knows. There's also Diana from Ffryes, my boyfriend, Peter, and Florence here in the office. So please don't think about making life difficult for me in my job here."

"I have no intention of doing so. I've admitted I got involved with Krasky's application and that should satisfy you. I would, however, be obliged if you and those you mention keep my involvement confidential."

"OK, so you have admitted your part. I won't make this public – on the understanding that you pay the money to Ettie."

"I can't do that. It's already gone."

"What! How the hell can you spend $10,000 in less than a week?"

"Because the money was not for me. I wanted it for my old church, St Andrew's Fellowship, near Liberta. It's one of the oldest churches in the parish and was damaged in Hurricane Lorna. The roof was virtually ripped off and they don't have any insurance or a big congregation to pay for repairs. The money will pay for a new roof. I've already donated a large sum myself and I've transferred the $10,000 to them. There was nothing in this business for me; I just wanted to see a first-class hotel being built at Ffryes. You know how important I think top-notch tourism is for the island. And to get the church fixed, well, that was a nice extra. I know I've been foolish, but in the end my cousin just did his job. He did nothing wrong."

Antonia sat in stunned silence. Without realising it, she had developed a strong dislike for Aaron: his lack of interest in cultural tourism and his cold-hearted part in the treatment of Ettie. But her anger subsided as she realised that Aaron was not such a bad man. His heart was in the right place. He cared about the financial prospects of the island and the importance of tourism, and at the same time he cared about his own small community.

"That… that's very interesting, but it still doesn't excuse you from a charge of taking a bribe. We can't be sure that your pressure on Elijah made no difference to the outcome of the applications." Antonia's tone was questioning, but not aggressive.

"I've never seen it as a bribe; it was a payment for my time. OK, it was a generous payment, but the Ffryes development will be a multi-million-dollar venture, so my fee was immaterial to Krasky. As I said, I'm certain the Land Registry's decision was a fair one and Elijah was never going to be swayed by me, was he? But Krasky didn't need to know that."

Antonia's temper was about to flare up again as Aaron tried to defend the use of fraudulent documents. However, she saw no point in going over the whole matter again. She took a couple of breaths to calm herself. "The end result is that Ettie has lost her family inheritance and the land now belongs to a US company. That's not what I would call a fair outcome – but since you haven't profited personally and there's no more that can be done about the ownership, that's the end of my involvement in this matter."

"You're not going to the police? You know that I have done nothing illegal."

"No, I will not, but be realistic, Aaron. You know the Land Registry will alert the police if fraud is suspected. I will not provide any information unless they ask me to, but I will be watching out for work being done at St Andrew's church. And you know my interest in island culture and history? I would like to restart discussions with you on cultural tourism. I have some new ideas I'd like to share."

"I've got no problem with that, but I need to give you some news that will be announced formally next week. Is Florence in the office just now?"

"Yes, I think so. Why?"

"Ask her to come in, would you?"

Antonia went out into the main office, quietly summarised their discussion to Florence and returned with her to Aaron's office. The door was closed and they sat down.

"Ladies, next week, the government minister for tourism will be making an announcement. Until then it's confidential, but I can tell you that I have requested early retirement from the ministry. I'm going into business with George Robartes, who, as you may know, is retiring from the water company. We're old friends and it's time we both wound down. We're opening a bar and café in Heritage Quay."

Florence spoke first. "Goodness, Aaron, that's a big change from what you have both been doing. Congratulations!"

Antonia was less impressed. "It's hard work running a bar."

"Yes, but we will be employing a chef and bartenders. We will really only be managing the bar in the background. And we will be ready for this season, as I only have one month's notice to serve here. The minister will be handling the appointment of a new director of tourism – he will mention that in the announcement next week. So, ladies, whatever ideas you have for the future of tourism in Antigua and Barbuda, you will have to discuss these with your new boss."

Antonia buzzed with excitement. Suddenly, she couldn't care less about Aaron and his bribe. She was certain that a new director would relish her cultural tourism ideas and at last she could look forward to a new start in her job – and she could point to something good coming out of the Ffryes business. She couldn't wait to get out of the office and call Peter to tell him the news.

"Well, I think that wraps up our discussion, Aaron," said Antonia. "We will say no more about the Ffryes affair."

Florence took the hint and they both stood and walked out of Aaron's office.

FIFTY-ONE

The following Wednesday, Antonia, Peter and Diana sat around the small plunge pool at Mike and Lisa's house in Tamarind Hills. Mike had brought out a tray of drinks and some nuts and olives.

"Thanks for coming at such short notice, everyone, but we thought it was important that we met without delay," said Lisa. "We heard about the outcome of the application for ownership at Ffryes Mills – everyone here at Tamarind Hills is worried about what will now happen to the area. But what we want to share with you is that I contacted one of my old friends at Lloyd's of London – she's one of the archivists there – and asked her to search for any details of the Cove Point insurance claim. I thought it might be possible to shed some light on what happened and the settlement details – just out of interest, really." Lisa turned to Mike and they both smiled broadly. "But something amazing has turned up."

"Are there still records relating to the claim?" said Antonia.

"Not paper records, but a few years ago a huge number of old files were digitised – those of special interest. Lloyd's are very proud of their three hundred years of history and have a sizeable archive team. There are records and artefacts going back to Nelson's day and even details of payments made following the loss of the Titanic. I asked my friend to see if they had images in the system for Cove Point. And guess what, they did! There's a report on the cause of the fire, how the boiling house was rebuilt, the cost and who the settlement payment was made to. And that's where the interesting bit comes in. All the repairs were arranged by Arkwright, initially out of his own pocket. With the agreement of the Lloyd's representative on the island, he went ahead with the work, not waiting for the money to come from the underwriters in London.

"Then, when the rebuilding was completed, he added to his claim what was described as a 'loss' at Ffryes Mills of £2,800. This must have been the market value of the Ffryes Mills estate at the time. There are copies of correspondence on this in the records, including a letter that states that Ffryes was sold to Nathaniel Foster and it seems that Arkwright was looking for compensation for the sale of Ffryes for just one pound. It's this aspect that made the case unusual. I've printed out some of the relevant pages."

"But surely that would not be covered by the fire insurance policy at Cove Point," said Peter.

"That's right – Arkwright was trying it on. His decision to sell to Foster for a pound was probably made spontaneously when he was feeling emotional after the rescue of his son and, as an afterthought, he tried to describe the financial loss of Ffryes as a direct consequence of the fire. He was never going to succeed on that front, but, look, this is the key letter on file." Lisa pulled out two of the sheets she had printed. "This is from the syndicate of underwriters, called C.P. Fotheringham and Others. I'll read out the relevant sections.

"*It is with regret that we must decline the element of the claim that relates to the loss in value at Ffryes Mills. While underwriters acknowledge the heroic action that Mr Nathaniel Foster exhibited in saving the life of the policyholder's son, and the consequent sale of Ffryes Mills by our policyholder (Mr Arthur Arkwright) to the said Mr Foster for the nominal sum of one pound, this loss of book value does not fall within the intention of the fire policy at Cove Point. The proposed settlement of £1,095 represents underwriters' liability solely for the expense of rebuilding the boiling house at Cove Point.*

"So, as far as trustworthy, impartial evidence goes, this is critical. You mentioned the Land Registry people wanted independent verification of the sale and I'm sure they will accept this letter as the proof they require, since it comes from Lloyd's." Lisa looked delighted with herself.

"And that's even though it's a photo image, the system Lloyd's uses to create the electronic archive meets all legal record-keeping requirements," said Mike.

Antonia clapped her hands. "That's brilliant, Lisa! We now have evidence of the sale to Nathaniel Foster that we can take to the Land Registry. I can't wait to tell Ettie."

Mike held up his hand to continue the story. "This information proves that the documents that claim the estate was sold in 1970 by the Arthur Arkwright estate to Caribe Landco are clearly fakes, because Arkwright's family didn't own the land at that time. The Land Registry people will no doubt ask the Antiguan police to look into the fraud that has been committed here by Ethan Krasky."

"Yes and he deserves all he gets," said Antonia. "Peter, would you come with me tomorrow? We should get this information to the Land Registry first thing so we can have their decision overturned."

"Sure, no problem."

"I'd be happy to come with you too, if you would like me to Antonia, to explain the Lloyd's records. Would that be OK?" said Lisa.

"Oh, thank you, that would be brilliant. Diana, on second thoughts, perhaps we should not tell Ettie about this until we know that we have been successful and the estate is hers?"

"I agree. No need to build her hopes up again. She is quite happy staying at my house for the time being."

***

Antonia phoned the Land Registry the moment the office opened to let them know they would be coming in at 10 a.m. to discuss new evidence in the Ffryes Mills case. The receptionist said Mr Trent was in the office, but she couldn't be sure he would be available for a meeting at such short notice. Antonia disregarded this; she was confident that once he heard why she wanted to see him, he would drop whatever he was doing and meet them.

With Peter and Lisa to give moral support, Antonia was shown into the same meeting room as before and given coffee. Andrew Jameson arrived to join them and explained that Mr Trent wouldn't be able to attend the meeting. Antonia slapped the Lloyd's documents down on the table. "Read these! They prove that Lee-Wind's application was fraudulent. I'd like you to review your decision on the Ffryes estate."

Jameson sat silently reading through the copies of the correspondence, his face growing pale, his fingers tremulously touching his lips. "Would you excuse me for one moment?" Without waiting for an answer, he stood up and hurried from the room.

They sat waiting patiently, but after twenty minutes, Jameson had still not returned.

"Bloody annoying that they should keep us waiting," said Lisa. She topped up their coffees.

Peter was more stoic. "It's a good sign; Jameson is no doubt trying to persuade Elijah Trent to come to the meeting. They will be shocked by this news, Antonia."

"I just hope they don't say they don't believe the Lloyd's papers."

"That's possible, but it would be very silly," said Lisa.

The door burst open and in strode Trent, with Jameson hurrying behind him. They sat down. Trent smoothed out the papers on the table in front of him and said, "Good morning. This is very disconcerting; a particular situation we have never experienced before in this department, under my management, at least. I have made copies of these papers and our legal team are considering them at the moment. However, knowing the credibility of Lloyd's of London, I am sure they will be verified as legitimate evidence of the sale of the estate by Arthur Arkwright to Mr Foster in 1892."

"And that means there is no way that the property could have been sold by Arkwright to Caribe Landco in 1970," said Peter.

Jaygo took a long, slow breath and nodded in reluctant agreement. "Yes, yes, that's true. We have a problem on our hands."

"What do you propose to do about it?" Antonia said firmly, wanting to keep the pressure on Trent.

"We will alert the police department and take steps to prevent any access to the site by Lee-Wind or people working for them. We will continue our enquiries and if the evidence is proven to be true, we will change our decision and find in favour of Miss Foster."

The door opened again and a smartly dressed woman came in with the copies of the documents and a notebook.

"What do you have for us, Amelie?" said Trent. "Amelie is our legal senior."

She consulted her notebook. "Well, sir, our document specialists examined these papers and they appear to be legitimate. I just came off the phone to Lloyd's of London – I spoke to a member of the archive team. They confirmed they carried out the research and issued the documents we have here. We therefore have no doubt that they are genuine and serve as proof of the sale of Ffryes sugar plantation and buildings, together known as Ffryes Mills, by Mr Arthur Arkwright to Mr Nathaniel Foster in 1892."

Antonia felt the warm glow of blood rise in her face and a smile form. It was impossible to hold back. "At last!" she said. "At last Ettie can have her property and no one will ever call her Mad Ettie again." Her smile broadened, as tears of happiness welled and rolled down her cheeks.

Peter took her hands. "Congratulations, my love, you have achieved wonders here for Ettie. I'm so proud of you!"

Antonia turned to Lisa and wrapped her arms around her. "It was Lisa who did the real work. Without your research at Lloyd's, we would never have been able to prove Ettie's ownership. Thank you so much, Lisa."

"My pleasure." Lisa hugged Antonia back.

Elijah Trent had recovered his composure. "Amelie, could you please ask the head of legal to contact the police and relate the facts of this case? I'm sure they will be keen to interview Mr Krasky as soon as possible."

"Certainly, sir, straight away."

"The next steps here will be the reversal of the registration of the property. I will need a magistrate to hear the case. I can ask for this to happen urgently. I would expect the court to sit by the end of this week. My team here will draft the documents to submit to the magistrate, confirming that Henrietta Foster owns Ffryes Mills. This will include liaising with the Civil Registry to confirm Miss Foster's succession to the family assets, but I'm confident that everything is in good order. There will be more papers for Miss Foster to sign, so could you bring her into the office as soon as possible?"

"Yes, no problem," said Diana.

"We are, of course, very concerned that the papers submitted by Lee-Wind Properties passed all our tests, yet some were fraudulent. But thanks to your efforts and belief, Miss Casey-Brown, the right outcome has been achieved. May I add my own congratulations?"

"That's very good of you, Mr Trent. Thank you so much," said Antonia.

***

Later that afternoon, there was a party atmosphere at Diana's bar and restaurant. Ettie laughed and chatted with all the guests, and even had a glass of champagne. Antonia barely let go of Peter's hand; the shock of almost losing him in the drama in the sea still reverberated through her mind and body.

Antonia saw Diana dash behind the bar, as one of the staff had called her to the phone. It was a short discussion and when she returned, she came straight over to Antonia and Peter, a look of puzzlement on her face.

"What is it, Diana?" Antonia wasn't in the mood for any bad news.

"That was Andrew Jameson from the Land Registry. He said that when the police arrived at Krasky's office in Falmouth this afternoon, they found it locked up and no one around. It was obvious that he had disappeared. They then called the airport authorities, who reported that Krasky departed on the lunchtime flight to Miami. It was either very fortunate timing on his part or Jameson thinks he could have been tipped off."

"Really? Who by?"

"Impossible to say. Could have been someone in the registry or a contact in the police department. I doubt that it will be possible to prosecute him in the United States and he would be a fool to set foot in Antigua again. I think we have seen the last of Mr Krasky."

"I wonder if one cousin spoke to another cousin after we left the office…" said Diana.

Mike nodded. "Could be, but the end result is that Krasky's now back in the US and out of reach of the Antiguan police."

"So he gets away with it, scot-free!" said Peter.

Antonia wore a wry smile. "Not entirely. The St Andrew's church rebuilding fund is $10,000 better off! And the Antiguan coastline will stay all the prettier in this area, with Ettie in possession of the land." She turned to Peter. "And I have the most adorable boyfriend that anyone could ask for."

The last rays of sunlight turned the sky into layers of pink and crimson as Antonia and Peter chinked their champagne glasses and kissed.

FIFTY-TWO

One year later

There was a tiny cloud over Montserrat in the distance, as the green-blue sea rhythmically rose and fell on the beach below. A pleasant breeze took away some of the heat and a row of canopies kept the guests out of the sun. Diana and Ettie had had their dresses handmade for the occasion: they were long and flowing, with a vibrant green and yellow abstract pattern for Diana and a plain red, white and blue for Ettie that could have been made from the flag of Antigua. They both had matching head scarves tied in a turban.

Lisa looked fabulous in a white trouser suit with a broad-brimmed fedora. Florence was stunning in a coral satin shift, a boater in a shade darker and matching white leather handbag and court shoes. It was a beautiful outfit but modest in cut; she knew it was poor etiquette to outshine the bride.

Right on 4 p.m. the wedding car arrived at the entrance to Sheer Rocks, just a minute's walk from the setting for the wedding ceremony.

All the guests were seated: Antonia's colleagues from the Ministry of Tourism, five of her favourite flight crew colleagues, Peter's work friends and golf partners, the couple's friends and family who had flown over from the UK. Antonia smoothed down her wedding dress. It was full-length, sleeveless and slim-fitting. She wore her grandmother's pearl necklace. Antonia waited for the wedding planner to cue the music, then started to walk down the aisle holding her father's arm. She breathed in the perfume from the roses and freesias in her bouquet. Peter stood at the far end, facing her, with his best man, Mike. They were both smiling broadly, wearing grey suits with white linen shirts, open at the neck; this wasn't the place to wear a tie.

Antonia couldn't hold back her delight. She wore a broad smile as she stepped onto the dais alongside Peter and the registrar. The breeze rustled the flowers in the pergola over their heads and the warm air was charged with the freshness of the sea. She felt sure there would be a wonderful sunset that evening.

The ceremony finished with one of Antonia's favourite songs, the beautiful 1940s ballad, 'The Waves on the Water', sung by Darius Delton:

The stars give us our future and
The moon shines on the waves on the water
My love will last forever
Like the waves on the water

The guests applauded when Peter led Antonia through the gardens to the Sheer Rocks restaurant, where their reception would be held. After everyone enjoyed a sumptuous meal and a steady flow of Caribbean cocktails, the steel band had them dancing until late into the night.

In the reverse of many honeymoon plans, the couple decided to take two weeks away from the Caribbean. They had booked a touring holiday in Scotland, starting in Edinburgh, then going on to Loch Lomond and the Isle of Skye and finishing at Gleneagles. But their departure from Antigua was three days away; first, they wanted to spend time with their family and friends, and show them around the island. Antonia particularly wanted her parents to meet Ettie and they arranged to have lunch the next day at Diana's restaurant. They would also have a tour of Ettie's new house, which was almost complete, sitting just off the road at the back of Ffryes, two minutes' walk from Diana's.

Ettie had agreed to sell a strip of land next to Tamarind Hills for the owners to extend their gardens and include a swimming pool for residents and guests, and this funded Ettie's house construction. She also sold a parcel of land at the back of the beach, near Diana's, to Antonia and Peter, so they could build their own house there. Despite their rigorous objections, Ettie insisted on selling the plot to them for one pound, just like old Mr Arkwright did for her great-grandfather, as a thank you for all they had done for her. Ettie gave the rest of the land to the Antigua national parks authority so they could preserve the area and renovate the windmill. A small visitor centre focusing on sugar plantations was built next to the windmill and the site had since become a popular destination for cultural tourism visitors to see. The bay was safe from redevelopment, and local residents and tourists alike continued to enjoy the beach, swimming, snorkelling and boat rides. Every Sunday, Ffryes beach was busy with families lunching; their barbecues smoking away all afternoon. Business at Diana's had never been so good. Ettie's story became legendary and she enjoyed her position as a local celebrity.

The Ffryes affair had ended as it should: with justice for Ettie and a loving future for Antonia and Peter.

ACKNOWLEDGEMENTS

Huge thanks to Mike and Lisa Duval for their very kind and generous hospitality (on more than one occasion!) at Tamarind Hills and for their review and comments on the storyline. I would also like to thank Ron Manser at Tamarind Hills and Simon Sherwood at Sheer Rocks for their agreement to feature their businesses in the book.

Thanks go to Flora Webber on behalf of Independent Talent Group, who represents Andi Oliver, for her efforts in securing Andi's approval of the reference to her in the story.

Jane Hammett completed the editing, and provided ideas and thoughts on the text that improved the focus and drama of the story. Thank you again for your excellent guidance.

As with *The Pearl River* and *The Berlin Assignment*, all the characters are fictitious but have elements of real people I know; family, friends and those I have observed from a distance. It has been fun developing the characters from those books into the grandchildren featured in The Ffryes Affair.

Special mention should be made of the Somerset Heritage Centre and the Somerset museum stored collections in Taunton, England, including an incredible assortment of original documents relative to sugar estates in Antigua. These feature accounts, sugar production, details of employees and the transport ships. The documents are retained in perfect condition and cared for with love and professionalism.

ABOUT THE AUTHOR

Born in London, but now living in Essex, Mark Butterworth worked in the City of London in financial services for nearly 40 years, including as a Lloyd's underwriter and risk management consultant. Travelling widely on holidays and business, often the two combined, Mark developed his appreciation of the Far East, Australasia, North America, the Caribbean and Europe. Mark held a Private Pilot's Licence for 15 years, including flights from Kai Tak and over the Sydney Harbour Bridge and Niagara Falls. Mark has flown a two-seater Spitfire and made more than 50 parachute jumps. Mark enjoys running, country walking, golf and salsa dancing and has two grown up daughters and a Springer Spaniel called Arthur. Mark has a BA from the Open University and an MBA from City University Business School.